She should go. She knew that. Her tattered heart was no match for this man's charisma. But the thought of going back to her lonely apartment just didn't appeal. Whether Trinity wanted to admit it or not, she craved the temptation Riley waved in front of her, even if he only offered it on a dare or some intoxicated high.

An escape, albeit temporary, from the deeply embedded loneliness that had taken hold of her soul from the moment her ex had dumped her so publicly at their hospital Christmas party two years ago and plunged her into depression and Scrooge-dom.

"Okay, Dr. Williams." She dug deep within her because she wanted what he offered. She needed what he offered. More than she'd ever realized. She would do this—would have fun. "I'll dance with you, but I should warn you that I dance much better than I kiss, so you might struggle to keep up."

She had no clue how she managed the confident words, or where they even came from, because seriously the only time she ever danced confidently was around her living room, with only Casper around to yawn at her antics. Still, head high, she headed back into the ballroom.

Riley's pleased laughter behind her warmed parts of her insides that hadn't seen sunshine in a long, long time.

Dear Reader

I am so blessed in that I come from a family where Christmas is always a special time and always has been. My family didn't necessarily get a lot material-wise, but the love and memories we have are worth more than anything a shiny package could ever hold. Sadly, I've run across people who have had a tragedy around the holidays, or who haven't been so blessed, and I think how terrible the holidays must be when there are reminders everywhere one looks.

Nurse Trinity Warren is just such a person. She's good-hearted, but grew up in a household where Christmas not only wasn't celebrated but also became an embarrassment for her, because her home life was so different from that of her peers. And getting dumped by her ex in a very public way at her hospital Christmas party sure didn't do anything to pump up her Christmas joy.

His name might not be St Nicholas, but Dr Riley Williams loves Christmas just about as much as the jolly red-suited man. Not used to being ignored by the opposite sex, Riley finds his interest piqued by Trinity's seeming indifference to him and her professed dislike of the most wonderful time of year. Showing her the magic of the season is the challenge his bored heart has been searching for, but can he really fall in love with someone whose life motto is bah-humbug?

I hope you enjoy reading Trinity and Riley's story as much as I enjoyed writing it. Drop me an e-mail at Janice@janicelynn.net to share your thoughts about their romance, Christmas, or just to say hello.

Merry Christmas!

Janice

AFTER THE CHRISTMAS PARTY...

BY
JANICE LYNN

First published in Great Britain 2013
by Mills & Boon, an imprint of Harlequin (UK) Limited.
Harlequin (UK) Limited, Eton House, 18-24 Paradise Road,
Richmond, Surrey TW9 1SR

© Janice Lynn 2013

ISBN: 978 0 263 23605 7

Janice Lynn has a Masters in Nursing from Vanderbilt University, and works as a nurse practitioner in a family practice. She lives in the southern United States with her husband, their four children, their Jack Russell—appropriately named Trouble—and a lot of unnamed dust bunnies that have moved in since she started her writing career.

To find out more about Janice and her writing visit www.janicelynn.com

Recent titles by the same author:

THE ER'S NEWEST DAD
NYC ANGELS: HEIRESS'S BABY SCANDAL*
CHALLENGING THE NURSE'S RULES
FLIRTING WITH THE SOCIETY DOCTOR
DOCTOR'S DAMSEL IN DISTRESS
THE NURSE WHO SAVED CHRISTMAS
OFFICER, SURGEON…GENTLEMAN!
DR DI ANGELO'S BABY BOMBSHELL
PLAYBOY SURGEON, TOP-NOTCH DAD

NYC Angels

These books are also available in eBook format from www.millsandboon.co.uk

Janice won The National Readers' Choice Award for her first book
THE DOCTOR'S PREGNANCY BOMBSHELL

Dedication

To my parents, James and Brenda Green, for making
all my Christmases so full of good times, good food,
and lots of love. Love you both very much!

CHAPTER ONE

IF THE PRETTY little blonde were a chameleon, Dr. Riley Williams was positive she'd have blended into the hotel ballroom wall long ago.

Who was she? Obviously not someone's date as only a fool would have left her alone. She had to be a hospital employee he just hadn't had the pleasure of meeting.

She sipped on a glass of what appeared to be rum punch and nervously surveyed the room as if she'd rather be anywhere than at the Pensacola Memorial Hospital Christmas party.

He took a sip of his soda and continued to listen to Dr. Sanders discuss an upcoming heart program the hospital was sponsoring while Riley's attention was really on the blonde.

Never had he seen a less likely wallflower. Although she did seem as delicate as one of the orchids his mother loved to grow. Fragile even.

Every bit as beautiful.

Looking almost hopeful, she smiled at a group of women that passed by but they never paused in their hee-hawing to say hello. If anything, she seemed to wilt further. A pity because he'd liked that brief glimpse of a smile.

The need to see that smile again hit hard. Surprisingly hard. He liked women. A lot. Always had. He imagined he always would but he didn't envision himself ever settling down. The long hours and demands of his career would keep him from ever tying a woman to him. A family deserved time and attention.

A plump pink lower lip disappeared between white teeth. Every muscle in Riley's stomach contracted and he'd swear the air in the room had thinned.

Never had he had such an instant, strong reaction to a woman.

He placed his half-full glass on a passing waiter's tray. "Excuse me, gentlemen, but I just spotted what I want for Christmas."

Several of his colleagues followed his line of vision and grinned.

"Trinity Warren. She just started last week," a cardiologist who was one of his partners informed him. "On the cardiac unit. I'm surprised you haven't already noticed her."

With the way his insides were stirring, so was he. Then again, he hadn't been around the hospital much this week. He'd taken a few days off work to spend some time helping his mother with odds and ends of Christmas decorations and shopping. For too long since his father's heart attack sadness had filled her at the holidays. Seeing her renewed joy in the festivities did Riley's heart good.

"Trinity Warren..." He let the blonde's name roll off his tongue, wondering at the way his pulse pounded at his throat. "She works on our unit?"

He didn't usually become involved with women he worked with. Too messy.

"She's been in orientation with Karen this past week. Quirky sense of humor, great smile, patients like her, seems to really know her stuff."

Yeah, well, he'd really like to know her stuff too. Up close and personal. Plus, that glimpse of her smile had been great. He could only imagine what her full-blown one would be like. His imagination was working overtime at the moment.

He studied her, watching as she cast her big brown eyes downward to stare into her glass before taking another sip. Her tongue darted out to lick punch from her full lips. He swallowed. Oh, hell. Without even trying, she was sending his blood pressure through the roof.

How much he wanted to see her pretty mouth curved into a smile stunned him, to see her eyes dancing with pleasure. Want was the wrong word. He needed to see her smile, her pleasure.

"You want me to introduce you?"

He glanced at his best friend and one of the several partners in their cardiology group. "Have you ever known me to need you to introduce me to a beautiful woman?"

"Figured you needed all the help you could get," Trey teased.

"Besides, I'm onto you," Riley continued, hesitating just a little longer, feeling his friend's interest in the woman too. "You're just looking for an excuse to talk to her yourself."

Trey grinned. "If I'd spotted her first tonight, I wouldn't have needed an excuse to talk to her. I'd be over there now, rather than talking to your ugly mug."

"But now?"

"Now I've seen the determined look on your face."

Trey shrugged. "She doesn't stand a chance and neither does any other man in this room. Go for it."

Relieved his friend didn't have a vested interest, Riley didn't deny his claim. Besides, Trey was right. Trinity Warren didn't stand a chance when he turned on the charm. Before long she'd be smiling and enjoying her evening—with him.

Nurse Trinity Warren was smart enough to know that facing her fears was the best way to move on, to put her ho-ho-ho hang-ups to rest. But, seriously, had she really had to come to this Christmas party?

Leaning against the hotel ballroom wall, she took a sip of her third cup of fruit punch. Was she nuts or what? By coming here, she was sticking her neck under the proverbial guillotine. Two years ago she'd vowed to never attend another Christmas party, to ban Christmas for ever. Bah, humbug! That had been her motto.

Only she'd relocated two weeks ago and her new nursing director had said she needed to attend. So here she was, pretending she was having a good time and that she wasn't contemplating a dash to the ladies' room to toss the liquid-only contents of her fluttery stomach.

She smiled at a group of women who worked in the billing department as they paused near where she held the wall up. She didn't personally know them. She knew very few people outside the cardiac care unit. But she had seen the trio around. Waving their hands with animation and talking a mile a minute, they didn't notice her.

"He is so hot," one of the women said, fanning her face with a bejeweled hand decked out with rakish long manicured fingernails and a sparkly ring so big it had to be fake.

"He's yummy in his scrubs, but in those dress slacks and fitted button-down open just right at his collar…" a heavy-chested blonde gave an exaggerated sigh "… he's outright lickable."

Trinity followed their line of sight to see who had their tongues wagging. Oh, my. Um, yeah, they were right.

He was hot.

And lickable.

And a lot of other things that had her looking away really fast so her retinas didn't start smoking.

Startled at her tongue-slurping reaction, she glanced back toward the object of their admiration. Her gaze collided with his. Wow. Something about him made her burn. Probably because he looked as if he'd walked straight out of every woman's fantasy. The mischievous gleam present in his blue eyes said he was well aware of his many manly charms and that she threatened to spontaneously combust any moment just from his visual perusal. He knew he was that hot.

She gulped back another sip of punch, hoping it would cool the burn. It didn't.

Which didn't make sense because she'd banned men right along with Christmas two years ago. Especially a man like the one grinning at her. A man like that one would incinerate the already shattered bits of her heart.

"Oh! Shh! He's coming this way," one of the women squealed, slapping the other's arm and sloshing a little of her Cosmopolitan onto the ballroom floor. All three of the women struck we-weren't-just-talking-about-you poses and one gave a fake laugh as if whatever they were discussing was of the utmost interest and batted her lashes flirtatiously.

Really? Trinity wanted to roll her eyes. She glanced Mr. Lickable's way again to see if he'd caught onto the women fan-girling him.

Yet again her gaze collided with electric blue and this time didn't let go, couldn't let go, as if there was some magnetic force at play that held her eyes in place.

She forgot how to inhale. Literally and figuratively. She couldn't breathe.

Wow. He really was a beautiful man. Dark brown hair that had just a touch of golden curl and looked invitingly soft. Tanned skin that hinted he spent a lot of his time outdoors and, living next to the Gulf of Mexico, he probably did. He had a face and body gorgeous enough to give any movie-star hunk a complex.

Then there were those eyes.

So intensely blue that they had to be contact lenses, because no one's eyes could really be that blue. Or that full of mischief. No doubt he'd been one of those kids who'd stayed on Santa's naughty list.

Yes, the women were right. He was hot, so hot her mouth felt like the Sahara but the rest of her rivaled a rainforest and was probably putting damp spots on her dress. Great. Managing to shift her eyes, she took another sip of her punch, draining the clear plastic cup. Oops. Now what was she going to do with her nervous hands?

"Do you want something else to drink?" Mr. Hotness himself asked, walking past the we-weren't-just-talking-about-you women and planting himself right in front of Trinity.

She glanced to either side, expecting to see some

parched Delilah close by. He couldn't be talking to Plain Jane her, right? And if he was, *why*?

The trio was staring at her in dropped-jaw surprise. She was surprised herself. She wasn't chopped liver, but she didn't kid herself that she was the model type this guy most likely dated either.

The last swig of punch had done nothing to help her dry mouth, which was problematic. Her tongue stuck to her palate, refusing to budge. She was positive anything she attempted to say could and would be held against her.

"I'll be happy to get you more punch," he added, causing a wave of eyebrow rises from their spectators. "Or anything else you might want." One corner of his mouth lifted in a sexy grin. "I'm a man who aims to please."

If the heavy-chested blonde had fallen into a fit of vapors right then and there, Trinity wouldn't have been surprised. She was about to need resuscitation herself.

He was flirting.

With her.

Eyes narrowing suspiciously, brain reeling, she peeled her dry tongue free of the roof of her mouth. "Then perhaps you should aim elsewhere."

Because, really, what would be the point of encouraging him? She wasn't interested in a relationship, or anything else.

Rather than take the hint and move on, his devilish grin widened, digging dimples into his cheeks. "You don't like to be pleased?"

Darn it. He was quick tongued and she'd set herself up for that one. No matter how she answered, he'd twist her words. The mischievous gleam in his eyes assured that.

She shoved her empty cup toward him. "Punch."

Fantastic. She sounded as if she had a mouthful of peanut butter and the IQ of a rock, but at least letting him get her punch would give her a reprieve.

Taking her cup, he laughed. "Then punch it is, but don't think I'm letting you off the hook. We'll discuss what gives you pleasure when I get back." His eyes sparkled. "I could make a few suggestions even."

Heat washed over her body, melting her from the inside out at the thought of just what those suggestions might be.

Not that it mattered. She so wasn't having that conversation with him.

"I wouldn't hold my breath if I were you," she mumbled.

She didn't meet his gaze and earn another laugh from him and an "Is she crazy?" from one of their billing-department eavesdroppers.

They probably thought she was, but the reality was that she didn't want to attract a man like him. Chase had been as high octane as she went and look where that had gotten her. Burnt. Burnt. Burnt.

"Who needs to hold their breath when you've already stolen mine?" he quipped with another flash of his perfectly straight pearly whites, sending her up in a puff of smoke. Then, in a decent imitation of a famous movie line, he added, "I'll be back."

The women sighed then giggled as if he'd said something super-romantic then brilliantly funny. Trinity just stared. Her gaze zeroed in on his retreating figure.

"You go, girl," the heavy-chested woman told her,

stepping closer and giving a thumbs up. "I'm pea green with envy. You're tonight's lucky girl."

She winced that the women had obviously overheard his pleasure comment. Great. She didn't want gossip. Lord knew, she'd dealt with enough of that during her lifetime already. Especially at work. And, seriously, although he was the hottest man she'd ever set eyes on, she didn't want a man in her life. Not ever again. Maybe she should leave before he returned. If her director got upset that she'd left too early, she could always claim she hadn't felt well. With her nervous stomach, she'd be telling the truth.

Glancing around, she easily spotted him in line to refill her punch and chatting with a few people whose faces she recognized but didn't recall which hospital department they hailed from.

Who was he and why had he sought her out?

What did it matter?

She was not getting involved. Especially not with someone who worked at the hospital or had anything to do with the hospital. Been there, done that, had the gaping hole in her chest to prove it.

A sick feeling took hold in her stomach, like she might really lose its contents. Time to go. Fast.

Eyes locked on the exit, she made a beeline for the ballroom door, intent on making her escape. Just after she stepped into the long hallway that would lead her to the hotel's over-decorated foyer, a hand grabbed her elbow. She jumped.

"You okay?"

Him. Great. No doubt there would be scorch marks where his fingers burned into her skin. She grimaced and started to say she was heading to the ladies' room, but why lie?

She turned, faced him, felt her breath hitch again at just how lickable he really was, then inhaled deeply because she was strong. "Look, I appreciate the offer of more punch and boring conversation, but I've had enough and I'm headed home."

His forehead creased. "You're leaving? Because of me?"

"No." Heat infused her face. Hadn't she just asked herself why she should lie? "Look, I'm not a party girl. You should go talk to someone else."

Understatement of the year.

"I don't want to talk to someone else. I want to talk with you. Besides, you're problem is that you've been partying with all the wrong people." His wink told her exactly who she should be partying with.

Determined not to be swayed by his outrageous charm and the way him saying he wanted to talk to her warmed her insides, she arched a brow. "I suppose you're my right person?"

A full-blown smile slashed across his handsome face. "I've been called a lot of things in my life, but I'm not sure Mr. Right is one of them."

She started to correct him, to let him know that she hadn't been implying that he was calling himself Mr. Right, but before she could, he reached out and ran a tingle-inducing fingertip across her cheek. Hello, light-ning bolt!

"There's always a first so, sure, I am the right person for you to be partying with tonight. I'm Riley, by the way." His smile cut dimples into his cheeks again and he stared straight into her eyes. "I don't want you to go."

Not offering him her name, she closed her eyes. It was all she could do not to lean towards him, be seduced by the appeal in his voice. Was he like the Pied Piper of women or what, because she just wanted to follow him wherever he led.

"Stay. Dance with me," he whispered near her ear in an enchanting tone that made her want to dance to his tune in more ways than one.

Mesmerized, she stepped towards him, her body almost pressing to his.

He inhaled. "You smell amazing. Good enough to eat."

Um, no. She was not going to let her mind go where his words threatened to take her. Not going to happen. Only her mind went exactly where it wasn't supposed to go. *Bad mind.*

Keeping her eyes squeezed shut, she parted her lips to say no, that she was leaving and couldn't be tempted by visions of sugar plums and whatever else he dangled in front of her. Apparently, he took her movement and open mouth as an invitation. Without hesitation his lips covered hers.

Shocked at the unexpected kiss, Trinity's eyelids flew apart, startled to find his intent blue eyes open, watching her, as his lips gently brushed over her mouth. Tasting. Tempting. Teasing. Rocking her world to the very core. Wow.

Shockwaves rippled to the tips of her toes and she questioned if time was standing still because the hotel seemed to fade away to just the two of them, just his eyes searching hers, his lips branding hers.

When he pulled away, reality immediately sank in. Hospital Christmas party. Surrounded by new coworkers. The most gorgeous man ever had just kissed her. Hello, had she lost her mind?

"Why did you do that?" She took a step back, wiping her lips as if trying to clear away his kiss. Sandpaper couldn't have erased his kiss. Riley. Riley's kiss. He'd permanently branded her lips, her entire body. The man started fires.

He pointed up to the doorway she'd stepped beneath.

"Had to." He shrugged nonchalantly, as if the kiss had been no big deal. To him it probably hadn't been. His knees weren't the ones shaking. "Tradition."

She glanced up, eyed the large clump of mistletoe tied with a red ribbon that hung over the doorway. Her gaze dropped back to him suspiciously. "You're a traditional kind of guy and just couldn't resist?"

"Absolutely, just ask my mom. She'll tell you I'm the apple of her eye." He grinned. "Now that we know I'm a traditional kind of guy, that you smell and taste like the sweetest candy, and the pressure of our first kiss is out of the way, let's go party. I guarantee a good time. Plus, you can tell me all about you while I hold you in my arms on the dance floor, Trinity." His eyes sparkled with devilment.

Feeling oddly out of sorts that he knew her name despite the fact she'd purposely not told him, that he was piling on the charm, she felt what little resistance she had to him ebbing away. "Do you always get what you want?"

One side of his mouth curved upward. "Not always, but it is Christmastime and I've been a very good boy."

She doubted that. Besides which there was nothing boyish about his broad shoulders and testosterone-laden aura.

"I'm hopeful there will be something sweet under my Christmas tree this year. An angel." He raised his brows. "You have plans? We could start a new holiday tradition."

She should go. She knew that. Her tattered heart was no match for this man's charisma. But the thought of going back to her lonely apartment just didn't appeal. Not even with Casper there, waiting for her. Her cat might love her but, whether Trinity wanted to admit it or not, she craved the temptation Riley waved in front of her.

An escape, albeit temporary, from the deeply embedded loneliness that had taken hold of her soul from the moment Chase Langworthy had dumped her publicly at their hospital Christmas party two years ago and plunged her into depression and Scrooge-dom.

Darn him for doing that. Darn her for letting him.

She took the punch glass Riley still held and downed half the contents as if she were chugging a shot of whiskey. Ha, she never drank alcohol, but she needed something to give her the push to do what she suddenly wanted to. She'd pretend the punch was liquid courage. She'd pretend that she was the kind of girl used to men like him flirting and wanting to dance with her. She'd pretend she was the life of the party.

"Okay, Riley…" She drawled his name out. She would do this, would have fun. "I'll dance with you, but I should warn you that I dance much better than I kiss so you might struggle to keep up."

She had no clue how she managed the confident words, the brilliant smile, or where they had even come from. The only time she ever danced confidently was around her living room with only Casper around to yawn at her antics. Still, head high, she headed back into the ballroom.

Riley's pleased laughter behind her warmed parts of her insides that hadn't felt sunshine in a long, long time.

CHAPTER TWO

WHAT A PLEASANT enigma, Riley thought of the woman he held loosely in his arms. She really did dance like an angel. But she was crazy if she thought she danced better than she kissed.

No one danced better than this woman's lips had felt against his. A meeting of their lips that hadn't been an angelic kiss but one that lit hot fires all along his nerve endings. He still burned. Of course, that might be because her curvy little body swayed next to his and every cell in him had an apparent surge of testosterone.

What other excuse could there be for that brief brushing of his mouth against hers to have set him on fire the way it had?

If he didn't quit thinking about how much he'd wanted to deepen that kiss, about how he wanted to take her somewhere private and kiss her again and again and on places other than her juicy mouth, she was going to know exactly what he was thinking. He was intuitive enough to recognize she wasn't the kind of girl who went for one-night stands.

And he wasn't the kind of man who sweet-talked a woman into doing something she'd regret.

Exactly what he did want wasn't entirely clear, but he sure wanted something.

Her.

He brushed his cheek across the top of her head, the light touch sending shockwaves of awareness through him. Yes, he wanted to know her in every sense. He'd always been the kind of person who'd known what he wanted and had gone after whatever that might be. He wanted Trinity with an intensity that made his head spin.

"How long have you been a nurse?"

Tilting her head back, she blinked her big brown eyes at him. Most of the women he knew would have had make-up accenting their large almond shape, would have made the most of the naturally thick lashes rimming her lids to lure some unsuspecting man into her snare. Not Trinity. As best he could tell, Trinity had nothing on her face except the light sprinkling of freckles across her nose and a little mascara coating those already long lashes. Her hair was clipped back with loose springs, framing her heart-shaped face. She looked as if she could be sweet sixteen.

"Trinity?"

Her beautiful face had become pinched, as if she were troubled by his question. "Long enough that I know about men like you."

Her instant defensiveness confused him. "Men like me?"

"You shouldn't get ideas about me." Her face flushed a pretty shade of pink, but she held his gaze. "I'm just here to dance, nothing more."

Riley liked the spunk shining on her upward-tilted face and had to fight the urge to kiss her mouth again.

"You shouldn't get ideas about me," he warned. "I'm simply making conversation with the beautiful woman I'm dancing with. Nothing more."

Her gaze narrowed. He grinned. After a moment she sighed in resignation. "Fine. You win." A sly smile slid onto her mouth. "This round."

He looked forward to future rounds. "And?"

"I've been a nurse for four years," she admitted, as if giving away some top secret. That would likely make her around twenty-six.

"Where did you nurse prior to coming to work for Pensacola?"

She tensed in his arms and stopped moving. "You don't have to play Twenty Questions or even make conversation at all. For the record, I'm a girl who appreciates silence in a man."

Riley chuckled. Oh, yeah, he liked this woman. "Shut up and dance, eh?"

She nodded.

"Problem is, I want to know more about you." Lots more. "Where did you nurse prior to coming to Pensacola?"

She sighed. "How about I save us a lot of time and send you a copy of my résumé?"

He stared at her stubborn expression.

"Oh, all right," she relented, and pushed his chest, motioning for him to start dancing again. "I went to school at University of Tennessee in Memphis and went straight to work at one of the hospitals there. I worked in the cardiac unit until I took the job here in Pensacola."

"Now, was that really so painful?"

"Excruciating." But a smile played on her lips. He

really liked her smile. And the sparkle of gold in her brown eyes.

"Now, be quiet and dance."

He laughed at her order. Talking with her was like a breath of fresh air. Stimulating. Fun.

"I have a friend who went to medical school in Memphis. He says it's a great place. What brought you to Pensacola? Family?"

With a look of what he hoped was feigned annoyance that he hadn't taken her order of silence seriously, she shook her head.

"Friends?" he persisted, despite her glare.

"Nope," she answered after a moment's hesitation.

The music picked up tempo. When she went to pull back he tightened his hold. "Boyfriend?"

"Ha. Exact opposite."

No hesitation there. He frowned. "You have someone in Memphis?"

"Not any more."

There was enough sadness—or was it regret?—in her voice that he felt a little guilty at just how much relief flowed through him at her denial.

"I'm glad there's not someone waiting for you in Memphis. Or anywhere else, for that matter." Because he hadn't liked the thought that she might belong to someone else. "Very glad."

For the first time since they'd started dancing she mis-stepped and caught his toe. "Sorry. I didn't mean to hurt you."

"You didn't," he assured her, thinking that as petite as she was she could stand on his toes and not hurt him. She was like a pixie. A curvy pixie. He couldn't recall ever having the urges that rushed through him when he looked at Trinity. There was something about her. Something intriguing that had him hooked. Was it just that she wasn't the type of yes-girl he was used to? "Recent break-up?"

She gave an ironic laugh and shook her head. "Forever ago. If you insist on talking, let's talk about something else. Anything else."

As much as he'd like to know more so he could understand what made her tick, Riley didn't push. Instead, he loosened his hold and caught her unawares by spinning her out and back to him. "Fine, we'll save the talking for later and dance now," he told her as he caught her.

Looking more than a little relieved, she smiled, then caught him unawares by dipping backwards in his arms and laughed as if she'd been set free. "Deal."

Trinity felt light-headed. Giddy almost. Despite her boisterous claim about her dancing skills, she stepped on Riley's toes more than once. He didn't seem to mind, just kept smiling at her and making silly little comments that made her laugh.

For once she relaxed enough to just enjoy the music, to let loose and move to the beat even if she looked ridiculous. Something about the way Riley looked at her, the way every bit of his attention was focused solely on her, boosted her confidence and let free her love of music.

Riley. He smelled so good. Spicy. Musky. Heavenly.

Her gaze dropped to his lips.

Somewhere in her brain she registered that something was wrong with her thought processes, that she wasn't thinking clearly. Still, she licked her lips, won-

dering if the flavor of him lingered there from his impromptu kiss. *She wanted to taste him again.*

"You're killing me, princess."

"Princess?" Had anyone ever called her princess?
And had she really just giggled?

A kiss under the mistletoe and a few fancy steps
to one of their coworker's karaoke singing "Rocking
Around the Christmas Tree" and she'd morphed into
someone she didn't even recognize. Who knew that pretending to be the life of the party could be so much fun?

"Well, you have me royally torn up so, yeah, princess." He grinned, his gaze going to her just-moistened
lips. "Don't tease me, Trinity."

He'd said her name. She liked him saying her name.
Her cloudy mind registered that she hadn't officially
introduced herself. "I'm Trinity, by the way." Which
seemed a really dumb thing to say as he'd called her
by her name repeatedly. She grimaced at her lapse and
wondered what was wrong with her brain.

He smiled indulgently at her. "Trinity Warren. I
know."

"How?"

"I asked about you before I came over."

She blinked, wondering if she'd misheard. "You did?
Why?"

His hand pressed against her lower back. "I wanted
to know more. I've never dated a woman who works at
the hospital. Too messy."

"Dated a woman who works..." Was he saying he
wanted to date her? Or just letting her know that he
didn't date women at the hospital so she wouldn't take
any of tonight the wrong way?

"Messy?" she prompted, then added, "Not that I'd date you."

He grinned at her comment. "I am going to prove you wrong but, yes, messy. If things don't work out, there's a mess to deal with when the two people involved work at the same place."

"Ha. Tell me something I don't know." She was an expert on that particular mess. Chase had worked as the IT manager for the hospital where she'd worked in Memphis. She knew all about dealing with messes. Especially when he'd made their break-up so public.

"You'll have to explain that comment," Riley commented close to her ear.

"Not likely." Because she had no intention of ever telling anyone in Pensacola of her humiliation. She'd come to forget things, not to rehash them.

His hold at her waist tightened a fraction. "You're a really private person, aren't you?"

None of her personal business had been private in Memphis. Chase had dumped her for another woman in front of the whole Christmas party. He'd been drunk and had… She grimaced, not letting the memories take hold. "Generally, I prefer to blend in than be center stage. If that means I'm a really private person, you're right."

He pulled back enough to stare into her face. "Funny, because when I look at you I can't picture you anywhere but center stage."

His kind words sounded so sincere that her knees threatened to buckle. She wanted to throw her arms around his neck and…actually, her arms *were* around his neck. She leaned closer, breathed in his musky scent.

He pulled back, stared into her eyes. "You're a lead-

ing lady, Trinity. You could never blend into the background."

Heat infused her face and she started to point out
that earlier tonight she'd blended in quite well until he'd
made an entrance into her life. Now lots of people were
looking at her and trying to figure out why he was dancing with her. Didn't they know? Tonight she was the life
of the party. Tomorrow she'd go back to the real world.

"You're smooth with the lines, Casanova."

His hand moved across her lower back, holding her
close. "No Casanova and no lines. Honest. I'm just telling you the truth. You're a beautiful woman."

"I think you're a player."

"You think wrong."

The woman's comment about her being tonight's
lucky pick ran through her mind. "You're telling me
you're as pure as snow?" She gave him a skeptical look.
"I'm not buying it."

"Not sure how pure snow is these days but no one
would label me as pure anyway other than my mother,
who thinks I hung the moon, of course." He winked.

Trinity rolled her eyes. "Okay, snowflake."

Her nickname obviously caught him off guard and
he stared at her a moment then shook his head, laughter shining in his eyes. "I enjoy spending time with
the opposite sex and I'm no saint, but you can call me
'Snowflake' if you want to. But for the record, I don't
say things I don't mean."

"No red-blooded man ever does."

"Suspicious little thing, aren't you?" He grinned.
"Fortunately, I'm an open book and you don't have a
quiz in the morning. So how about for the rest of the
night you don't analyze this and just enjoy yourself?"

"With you?"

He tightened his hold at her waist. "That was the idea. I'd be very disappointed if you left me to enjoy yourself with someone else."

Despite her uncertainty, the giddy feeling was still inside her so she just shrugged as if she couldn't care less one way or the other. "So long as you don't suggest we sing karaoke."

That naughty look twinkled as brightly as the colored lights adorning the Christmas tree in the corner of the ballroom. "Too bad, because my number is coming up two songs from now and I plan on you joining me."

"You plan wrong."

He reached into his dress pants pocket and pulled out a slip of paper. "Due to the time constraints, the Christmas committee had interested parties draw numbers earlier this evening." He waggled his brows. "This interested party got a winning number."

"I'd ask if you ever don't win, but having to get up in front of all these people and sing doesn't sound like a prize." Grimacing, she glanced at the duo currently belting out a number. "Not a good one, at any rate."

He laughed and touched his finger to her nose. "You're funny, Trinity. I like that."

"Not really." She wasn't funny. She hadn't been since…since Chase had broken her heart and she'd withdrawn into her shell, trying to protect her tender inside.

Why had she done that? Why had she let him steal so much from her? Why was she still letting him steal so much of her life? For goodness' sake, she had moved to a beach town because she'd assumed the locals wouldn't put so much emphasis on a holiday associated with snow. Pathetic.

"Fine, I'll sing with you, but just to warn you, I'm an even better singer than I am dancer and we both know how I excel at that." She stepped on his toes, hard, to prove her point.

"My ears can hardly wait." He grinned down at her. "Like I said, fun girl."

CHAPTER THREE

TRINITY'S HEAD HURT. Not just a little. Her mouth felt as if something had crawled inside and died. Her stomach warned she might just upchuck.

She rarely ever got full-blown, miserable sick, but this morning she just felt bleh. Thank goodness she wasn't scheduled to go into work today, just to take call. Maybe she'd get lucky and her phone wouldn't ring.

Digging deeper beneath her covers, she groaned and snuggled up next to the warm body beside her.

Warm body? Hello. There wasn't supposed to be a warm body in her bed!

"Good morning, sleeping beauty," an unexpected voice broke into her haze.

An unexpected and very male voice.

A voice she immediately recognized, even though she'd only met him the night before. Why was he rambling on about sleeping beauty being a princess and her looking like one? Right. Because, like all fairy princesses, her hair and make-up remained perfect while she slept. *Not.*

She twisted to look at him. "Riley."

"You were expecting someone else?" A lazy brow rose beneath sleep-tousled hair and he looked way too sexy for first thing in the morning. Apparently fairy princes really did remain perfect while sleeping.

She was in bed. Her bed. Between the covers. With Riley. Her heart pounded against her ribcage. Not good. She scooted away from his warmth until she reached a cold spot on the sheet. Too bad half her butt was now hanging off the edge of the bed.

"I wasn't expecting anyone." Her words came out half-croak, half-cry.

Pulling the covers tighter around her, she tried to register the fact that she was in bed with Dr. Riley Williams. Even more confusing, she tried to remember how she'd gotten there. How he'd gotten there.

"What are you doing here? You shouldn't be here."

He shouldn't. She barely knew him. She didn't do one-nighters. Not ever. She didn't do anything. Not before or after Chase.

At her accusing tone, Riley's grin slipped. "You asked me to stay."

That threw her. "I did?"

"You did." His confident tone and coolly assessing blue gaze brooked no denial.

She'd asked him to stay. They were in her bed. Although her black dress was gone, as were her hose, she still wore her panties. But no bra.

In bed with a sexy cardiologist with nothing on but her granny panties. Awesome.

She closed her eyes, took a deep breath and asked the twenty-million dollar question that kept echoing through her throbbing head.

"What did we do?" She sounded accusatory again, but she wasn't able to control the rising panic within her.

What had she done? She'd finally broken away from

the chains that had bound her to Memphis, had moved to Pensacola to make a fresh start, and she'd ended up in bed with the first man she'd stood under mistletoe with? How could she?

Christmas.

It was the blasted holiday that wreaked havoc in her life. Always had. Always would. She really should go to some remote location every December and not come home until well after New Year. If only.

Riley had the nerve to look offended. "You don't remember last night? Our coming here? What we did after we got here?"

"If I remembered, would I be asking?" Really, she'd thought him smarter than that. Or maybe she was just cranky because a thousand things were running through her mind and not one of them good. "Did we have sex?" she demanded, while her throat still worked because, seriously, the tissue threatened to swell shut any moment.

From where Riley lay next to her, he stared, not saying anything at first, just watching, making her wish she could pull the covers over her head, making her wish her stomach didn't churn.

"I can assure you—" confidence and perhaps annoyance oozed from his words "—that had we had sex, you'd not only remember, you'd have woken up with a smile on your face and not that look of horror."

Face aflame, relief flooded her, as did curiosity because sex up to that point in her life hadn't been that memorable. There had just been Chase but, still, she had been practically engaged to the man. Sadly, she had never woken up with a smile on her face. Quite the opposite. So maybe Riley thought she'd remember if they'd had sex, but maybe she wouldn't have remembered. Maybe she just hadn't been impressed and had blocked the experience from her mind.

"You're saying we didn't, um, you know?"

Cool amusement at her lack of ability to say the actual words shone in his eyes. "We didn't have sexual intercourse last night, if that's what you are attempting to ask."

No sexual intercourse. His tone mocked her question but, come on, they were in bed and she was only in her skivvies. Which meant that they had done something, right? The way he was looking at her said they'd done something. But what?

Letting her gaze run over his face, his lips, the strong line of his jaw, his throat, his bare shoulders, his chest, his... She gulped. Had she touched him? Kissed him? Run her fingers over those broad shoulders? Those washboard abs? Had she seen him naked? Face afire, she glanced back up, met his gaze, and winced. He so knew what she was thinking and he liked it.

An inferno burned her cheeks.

"Riley, I..." She pulled the covers even tighter around her, holding on in case the material got a sudden urge to slip below her neck and put her chest and abs on display for his inspection. No washboard anywhere in sight at her midsection. More like a laundry basket. Taking a deep breath, she tried to pull her thoughts together and away from their bodies. "I don't do this."

"This?" His face was unreadable, his eyes dark. She didn't like the look and found herself wishing things were different. That she was different. That she could have woken up in bed with him and not freaked out but reveled in a night full of passion. That she really had woken up with a smile. That she could have been good enough that he could have woken up with a smile. That instead of lashing out at him with accusatory questions she could have teased him awake with kisses and had a morning full of passion.

A morning she'd remember always.

A morning he'd always remember.

A morning that would leave them both exhausted and smiling.

But that wasn't her. She was a woman who disliked Christmas, disliked men, was terrible at sex, and although she'd come to Pensacola to forget her past, she could only handle confronting one hang-up at a time. She seriously had her work cut out for her even with that.

"What is it that you don't do?" Riley prompted when she failed to elaborate.

Everything. She sighed, took a deep breath and went for broke.

"Wake up in bed with a man and not remember how I got here and what we did while here." She grimaced. She sounded horrible. Waking up next to him was horrible. He probably thought she was horrible—in bed and out of it. "I don't do that. Ever."

"I just told you, we didn't do anything, not really. We ended up here because I drove you home from the Christmas party and you invited me in. And, although there's another bedroom, there is no bed."

Which meant he must have at least considered sleeping elsewhere.

"I wasn't doing the floor," he said matter-of-factly, "and I'm too tall to comfortably sleep on your girly sofa."

She did have a girly sofa. A plush Victorian piece

that she loved because it had been the first piece of furniture she'd ever bought for herself, but it really wasn't that comfy. Not that comfort mattered so much, because she never had company or spent much time there.

Trying to recall the previous night's events, she closed her eyes, thought back. The Christmas party. She'd danced with Riley, sung one silly reindeer song with him, celebrated that he'd won one of the door prizes when random names had been drawn from a stocking, then they'd left. He'd driven her home. They'd walked into her house and then he'd kissed her. No mistletoe required. Just a simple good-night kiss that had somehow morphed into something more, something hotter, something that hadn't been simple at all.

Wow, if his kiss had been that amazing she might have really woken up with a smile had they had sex. Then again, had they had sex he'd know how lame her lovemaking actually was.

Her panties weren't the only thing she was wearing.

She reached up, touched the door prize he'd won and given to her. "You won this."

He shrugged, causing the covers to slip a little lower at his waist. "I gave it to you."

He'd taken the pearl necklace out of the velvet box and fastened it around her neck. There had been something mesmerizing about him putting the necklace on her. Something erotic and gentle and totally captivating.

Kind of like his abs.

No wonder she'd asked him to stay. He'd been the perfect date.

Only they hadn't been on a date.

"You can have it back if you want it," she offered, in case he regretted having given her the piece. Maybe he'd expected bodily payment for the beads. Ha, had they been out of a gumball machine he might have gotten his money's worth, but that's about it if Chase's claims about her skills could be believed.

Riley's brows formed a V. "Why would I want them back? Don't you like the necklace?"

"It's lovely."

"Not nearly as lovely as you are."

He was smooth with the lines. Too smooth perhaps. She swallowed.

"You told me I was beautiful last night."

Actually, he'd repeated the compliment several times.

"You were." His eyes bored into hers. She didn't have to be looking directly at him to feel his stare. He stirred beneath the covers, but he didn't reach for her. Somehow she knew he wanted to.

"You are," he continued. "Very beautiful."

Last night, in her haze, he'd made her feel beautiful. Like the most beautiful woman in the world. This morning she felt like a woman who'd gone to bed without washing her face or brushing her teeth. She was rank and knew it.

"Why would you say that?"

"Because it's true."

The sincerity in his voice told her that he was either the world's greatest liar or he believed what he said. Maybe he really did have fantastic blue contact lenses and they were blurred with sleep, leaving him blinded to the truth.

Making sure to keep the covers pulled over her almost bare body, she rolled over to face him directly. She could feel his body heat, could feel the magnetic pull of him. She wanted to touch. Really really wanted to touch. His sheer physical perfection robbed her of thought. Or maybe it was his bare chest that made her brain waves frazzle. He was the one who was beautiful. Eye-poppingly, mouth-wateringly, finger-itchingly, body-twitchingly beautiful.

It occurred to her that the happy trail leading beneath the covers didn't appear to have anything material impeding its path. At least she was wearing underwear.

No sexual intercourse, he'd said. That left a lot of possibilities. Oh, my.

"What happened to your clothes?" she choked out, more and more flustered that he was naked in her bed.

Although she recalled the removal of her clothes, she didn't recall how he'd gone from fully dressed to whatever he still wore beneath her covers.

He was wearing something. *Wasn't he? Just because she couldn't see any outlines, it didn't mean boxers or cotton briefs weren't there, right?*

His eyes glittered. "You don't recall ripping them off me with your teeth, princess?"

She'd taken them off him? With her teeth? Her jaw dropped then clamped shut in case her teeth got any fresh ideas.

"Okay, it was bad of me to tease you." His grin turned devilish. "You didn't use your teeth."

She'd... She closed her eyes and tried to recall the events of the night before. "We had sex, didn't we?"

"I already told you that we didn't have sex." He sounded annoyed that she'd asked again, that she hadn't taken him at his word.

Unable to resist a moment longer, she reached out beneath the covers to touch his chest. His bare chest. To see if the feel of his skin was familiar, to see if touching him would cause a rush of memories.

"Then why are we naked in my bed?"

"I wasn't planning to spend the night anywhere so I hadn't packed any pajamas…not that I normally wear anything to bed. But I'm not naked. I'm wearing boxers and would be happy to show you if you'd like proof." He covered her hand with his, brushed his thumb across her skin. "Besides, you looked as if you needed me to stay. My guess is that you don't drink often."

Still reeling from his offer to show her his underwear and just how tempted she was to take him up on that offer, she focused on the other part of what he'd said. "I don't drink at all and I didn't drink anything last night except fruit punch."

"That was rum punch you were drinking, Trinity. It had alcohol in it."

"The punch was…but…" Hadn't she felt funny? Hadn't she noticed that the more she'd drunk the less nervous she'd been? *Dear Lord*. "I was punch drunk."

Looking as if he wanted to laugh, he just grinned. "You were a bit inebriated but no worries, you were a cute drunk."

A cute drunk. As if such a creature existed. No one was a cute drunk. At least no one Trinity had ever had the misfortune of seeing drunk. Her mother had certainly never been cute. Chase had not been cute.

"I didn't know there was alcohol in the punch."

"It's okay, princess." His thumb paused and he gave her a sympathetic smile. "I figured out that you weren't at a hundred percent. That's why nothing happened."

She tried again to remember the events of the night

before, but only bits and pieces came back to her. "You wanted something to happen?"

He gave her a look that questioned if she had really asked that. "Of course I wanted something to happen."

"Why?"

He laughed but the sound came out a little stilted. "That's a question with a very obvious answer."

"Because you're a guy?"

"Despite what the female population may believe, not every guy wants sex to the point of doing so with any willing woman."

Which meant she'd been willing but he hadn't been. Urgh. What was she thinking? Of course she'd been willing. The man was hot and got under her skin to probe places she'd rather keep locked away. She'd been under the influence to where her fears wouldn't have come into play to remind her of yet another reason why she should keep her legs closed.

"I'm confused. You wanted something to happen, but even though I was willing, nothing happened?" Even as she said the words, the reality that they were almost naked, lying in her bed, hit her. That he could have taken advantage of her and he hadn't. She liked that. A lot. Possibly because most of the men in her life had taken advantage at every opportunity presented. Not sexually, necessarily, but in any other way they could.

Riley made a sound that she wasn't sure was a low laugh or a growl. "Yes, princess, I wanted something to happen. A lot of somethings. Had you been sober, this morning would have been very different."

She didn't doubt that the morning would have been different. Had they had sex, he probably would have snuck out at some point during the night. Or perhaps he wouldn't have bothered to sneak, he'd have just gone, and left her to her non-sexual self. She knew her strengths and weaknesses and if she hadn't, Chase had done a really bang-up job of pointing them out to her and anyone else who had cared to listen. Sexual prowess wasn't in her bag of tricks.

"I'm sorry."

"I don't want you to be sorry," he surprised her by saying. "What I want is to see you smile."

She bared her teeth in a semblance of a smile because, really, he deserved a smile. He was unlike any man she'd ever known and that made her want to know more…and terrified her, too.

"Not exactly what I had in mind, but it's a start." He smiled so warmly at her that the nausea within her actually eased. "Now, the most pressing question is whether you have any food in this joint so I can cook us something or would you like to go out for breakfast? I'm starved."

In reality they did neither. Not long after she'd draped the comforter around her shoulders and rushed into her bathroom to clean up her mess of a face, he tapped on the door.

She cracked the door open to peer at him. He was fully dressed in his clothes from the night before.

"I've got to head to the hospital. I'm on call today, and they've had several chest pains come into the emergency room. Apparently the cath lab is a madhouse. Dr. Stanley is going to be tied up there for some time and there are two more chest pains on their way by ambulance."

Trying not to look too disappointed that whatever

their morning had been going to bring had been interrupted, she nodded. "I understand."

Apparently she didn't do such a good job at hiding her doubts.

He tilted her chin toward him so he could fully see her face. "For whatever it's worth, I don't want to go."

His fingers on her face were so warm, so tender that she sucked in her breath. "What is it you want?"

"To spend the day with you. Maybe help you drag out your Christmas decorations because your apartment is sadly lacking in Christmas spirit. Or, for that matter, we could decorate my tree. It's been delivered, but I haven't had a chance to trim and decorate it."

He had a live Christmas tree? Who did that in these days of commercialized Christmas? Not that she'd be doing either of his suggestions. She'd had her fill of Christmas spirit the night before and preferred to stick her head in the ground until the season passed. Just look what happened when she tried to get into the spirit of things. She'd ended up drunk and waking in bed with a man she barely knew. No, thank you.

"Honestly, what we did wouldn't matter so much just as long as I got to spend some time with you."

From somewhere in her bedroom her cellphone started buzzing.

"If that's who I think it is, you'll probably get your wish. I'm on call today, too, and if you've been called in, I'm likely to be as well," she mused, pulling her robe tight around her while she dashed toward where her phone had ended up the night before.

"The hospital?" he asked the moment she disconnected the call.

She nodded.

"Maybe the chest pains will end up gastro related rather than cardiac and we won't have to stay long. We could grab lunch," he suggested.

"Maybe," she replied, dropping the phone back into the small black evening bag she'd carried the night before.

"Trinity?"

She glanced towards him.

"I like you."

She wasn't sure what to say.

"I'd like to see you again."

Was he a glutton for punishment or what?

"Despite whatever impression I gave you last night, I'm really quite boring," she said, wondering if she should also warn him about how much baggage she carried. The airport's claim area had nothing on her.

"I don't believe you."

"You should," she warned. "I've known me a lot longer than you have."

He laughed then glanced at his watch. "I could never be bored around you, funny girl. Unfortunately, I have to get moving and your car is still at the hotel where the Christmas party was held. You'll have to ride with me to the hospital so get hopping. We have lives to save."

"Sure thing, snowflake."

CHAPTER FOUR

ALTHOUGH RILEY HADN'T been on the schedule, he still spent most of the day at the hospital.

Fortunately, so did Trinity.

He'd been able to easily maneuver her into the cardiac lab with him. Right or wrong, he wanted her near him. The panic he'd seen in her eyes that morning worried him. Plus, she was going to need a ride to pick up her car at the end of her shift. He was way too smart to miss out on the opportunity to play white knight and give her a lift.

Doug Ryker, a fifty-three-year-old, had woken up with chest pain that had increased as the sun had come up. When he'd started clutching his chest, his wife had called 911. An ambulance had brought him to the emergency room. His cardiac enzymes had been elevated and, at the minimum, he'd needed an arteriogram.

That's where Riley came in.

He'd met the gentleman's family very briefly while the patient was being prepped. Now Riley was scrubbed and ready to proceed. Trinity was his nurse.

He stole a look at her. If she noticed, she ignored him and focused on their patient.

Too bad there wasn't a sprig of mistletoe around because he'd love to pull down her mask and kiss those plump lips of hers. Did she remember their kiss beneath the mistletoe or had she blocked it from her mind along with the rest of the night? Just how much did she remember about their evening together?

'Twas the season for good tidings and cheer. Riley couldn't think of anything that would cheer him more this Christmas than getting to know the lovely woman he'd spent the night holding and had developed a fascination for that he couldn't quite explain, much less understand. Maybe it really was the season?

He loved Christmas, everything about it. The sounds, the smells, the spirit of giving, all of it. If someone popped a bow on top of Trinity's head and set her beneath his tree to unwrap, he'd be a very happy man.

He glanced over at the angel monitoring Mr. Ryker's vital signs.

She caught him looking. Instant hot pink tinged what he could see of her upper cheeks peeking out from behind her surgical face mask. He winked and her color deepened.

Something warm and fuzzy, like the smell of cookies baking, filled him. Something that just made him feel…happy.

Odd that the feeling felt strange, because he couldn't think of anyone he'd label as happier than him. He was totally happy go lucky. Yet he couldn't deny that the feeling felt alien.

And addictive because already he knew he'd want more when the feeling waned.

Maybe everything would go well with Mr. Ryker's arteriogram and the man wouldn't need anything beyond a few stents. Then, Lord willing, Riley would ask Trinity to go to a late lunch.

"Vitals are good," she said, probably more just to say something rather than to actually inform him.

After she'd prepped Mr. Ryker's groin, Riley numbed the area with an anesthetic and made a penciltip-sized incision. Carefully, he threaded the cardiac catheter through the femoral artery and up into Mr. Ryker's heart.

Mr. Ryker's elevated enzymes had already conveyed that there was cardiac tissue not getting proper perfusion. Riley had hoped he'd find a single small blockage that could be fixed easily with a stent to restore blood flow. He found much more than that. Unfortunately.

Mr. Ryker's mammary artery had a large area of calcification and stenosis. Plus, there were other areas of calcification scattered throughout the arteries. Riley carefully positioned the catheter tip and placed a stent, then another, corrected the blockages that he could via an artificial material holding the artery open. Unfortunately, the stents weren't nearly enough to restore blood flow to the tissue. He withdrew the catheter.

"He's going to need a coronary artery bypass graft," he told another nurse, while Trinity applied pressure to where the catheter had been withdrawn. "Find an available vascular surgeon stat and let's get Mr. Ryker into the operating room."

So much for taking Trinity out to eat any time soon. They'd be here for several hours yet.

Trinity wasn't sure how she'd gone from being in the catheter lab to the operating room as that wasn't usual protocol. At least, it hadn't been standard at the hospital where she'd worked in Memphis, but there she was. In the operating room. With Riley.

She was working as his assistant and blowing CO_2 into Mr. Ryker's open chest. That helped keep blood from interfering with Riley being able to readily see where he was making the anastomosis in the mammary artery to loop the vessel into the right coronary artery. While keeping the CO_2 blowing at just the correct angle, she watched him carefully cut away a pedicule and reroute the artery. Painstakingly, he sutured the arteries together, making sure not to damage the vessels.

Another nurse dabbed at his forehead. Trinity found herself wishing she was the one touching him. Silly really. They were at the hospital. Working to save a man's life. Touching the cardiac surgeon while he performed a procedure should be the absolute last thing on her mind.

She'd touched him the night before.

On the lips under the mistletoe and again on the dance floor and again this morning when she'd reached out to touch his magnificent chest. Who knew where else she'd touched him during the night? After all, she'd woken up spooned against that long, lean body of his.

She swallowed back the knot forming in her throat and refocused her attention on the CO_2.

After what seemed like hours she snuck a peek. His blue eyes, which were normally so full of mischief, were focused intently on the job at hand, on how he meticulously placed sutures, making sure the vessel remained patent, that every movement of his hands were precise.

He'd been full of fun and teasing the night before, and even this morning. Now he was as serious as serious could be. Which one was the real him? The mischievous player who'd stolen a kiss from her under the mistletoe or the brilliant, intense heart surgeon attempting to save his patient's life?

"How late do you have to stay?" Riley asked Trinity later that day, hoping she wouldn't have to pull a full shift.

"I'm not sure. If nothing else has come into the emergency room, I expect the charge nurse will let me go soon." She gave him a suspicious look. "Why? Do you need me to help you with something? Another procedure?"

"I do need your help with something. Have dinner with me."

Her brow lifted. "You need help with dinner?"

"I'll be lonely if you don't join me."

"I seriously doubt you're ever lonely."

He thought about her comment. He couldn't really say that he recalled ever being lonely. He had a full life that he enjoyed a great deal, but the thought of not spending the evening with Trinity, as crazy as it was, did leave him feeling oddly bereft. "You might be surprised."

"I don't think going to dinner together is a good idea."

Why had he known she'd refuse? "Because of last night?"

Her cheeks blushed a rosy pink and she shook her head.

"No?" One eyebrow rose. "Because you don't want to encourage an incorrigible bloke like me?"

Looking torn, she took a step back. "That's not it."

He waggled his brows. "Then you *do* want to encourage an incorrigible bloke like me?"

If her cheeks had been pink before, now they were blood red. "You are incorrigible, but…"

He took her hands in his. "Then you'll help me?"

"You don't understand."

"You have other plans?"

"No, but—"

"No worries, I'll let you choose where we go. I'll even splurge for dessert."

"I don't want dessert."

He shrugged. "Okay, I'm easy. No dessert for you. If you're nice I'll share mine, though."

She let out a long breath. "You really are incorrigible."

He wouldn't deny it.

"What time should I pick you up? You need a ride to your car and it's my responsibility to get you there."

"I'm not your responsibility."

He studied her a moment then rubbed his knuckles across her cheeks. "We're talking dinner and a ride to your car, Trinity, not for ever. Smile and say, 'Thank you, I'd love to go to dinner with you, Riley.'"

Her face screwed up with doubts, she bared her teeth. "Thank you. I'd love to go to dinner with you, Riley."

He laughed and tweaked her nose. "Atta girl."

How had Riley finagled Trinity into doing this?

Going to the hospital Christmas party one night and going on a dinner date the next was just too much for her bah-humbug to digest.

Oh, yeah, she didn't have her car, she justified to herself.

"Jingle-bells, jingle bells," he sang, looking way too

amazing in his jeans and lightweight sweater as he maneuvered through traffic.

Urgh. The only thing worse would be if he was wearing an ugly Christmas sweater.

He glanced her way and grinned. "Penny for your thoughts."

"You don't want them."

"Sure I do."

"I was imagining you in an ugly Christmas sweater. I bet you have a closet full."

Laughing, he arched one brow. "Ugly Christmas sweater?"

"You know, the ones that sport more decorations than a department store."

"Oh, those ugly Christmas sweaters." He grinned. "I might have a few prime specimens tucked away from years past. You wanna borrow one, or are you just making your Christmas gift request?"

"Hardly." But she ruined the effect by laughing at the thought that he might really have a few. Surely not. Covering his shoulders and chest with a knit sweater with sparkly dangly things all over it would be awful.

"Speaking of department stores, do you mind if we swing by and pick up a few strands of lights for my tree before we go eat? I should have grabbed some last week but didn't realize mine were shot at the time."

She bit the inside of her lip. He'd been so kind to her that could she say no?

"I guess that would be okay."

Not really, but maybe she could sit in the car to avoid the hustle and bustle. If he insisted on her going inside the store, she could surely find a happy place in her mind somewhere for however long it took him to get his lights.

"Don't sound so enthusiastic," he teased.

She didn't want to seem ungrateful. He'd transformed the night before into a fun memory…at least the parts she remembered had been fun. He'd not taken advantage when she'd been at his mercy. He'd been gracious and kind, offering to take her to dinner and to get her car. He made her smile. Whether she wanted to or not, she liked the man.

"Sorry, I guess I get a little cranky when I get hungry."

Pulling into a parking spot, he turned off the ignition and reached across the car to take her hand. "If it's okay, I'll do a quick run for the lights while you grab us some sandwiches from the place there." He handed her a couple of twenties and pointed to a sandwich shop. "I'll make it up to you by taking you to my place so you can help decorate my tree. Deal?"

Before she could tell him that decorating his tree would be more like punishment, he got out of the car. "I'll take a club loaded with everything…hold the onions."

A sinking feeling in her gut, Trinity watched him rush toward a seasonal store in the strip mall.

Dinner and decorating a tree? Not what she'd signed up for, but apparently what she'd be doing, all the same, with a forced smile for Riley's sake.

Trinity had to admit the sandwiches were delicious or she really had been hungrier than she'd thought. The tree decorating, well, she was still holding back her opinion on that.

Not that she enjoyed the decorating but she'd have to be blind not to appreciate the view. Standing on a stepladder, Riley leaned and made another snip from the live blue spruce tree that towered several feet over her head. After clipping a few more twigs, he inspected the tree to see if it met with his approval.

From where she stood at the bottom of the ladder, she had to admit he definitely met her visual approval. The man was hot.

"What do you think? Look good?"

Did he have a crystal ball to see into her mind or what? "Oh, yeah."

"Now, that's the enthusiasm I've wanted to see all evening. To think, if you'd had your car you'd have found some excuse to say no."

Trinity closed her eyes and winced. He'd meant the tree, not his rear end. Duh. Of course he hadn't meant his rear end.

"I did say no," she reminded him. The man was persuasive. She'd better be careful or he'd have her agreeing to dress up in a red suit and climb down a chimney proclaiming, ho, ho, ho and a merry Christmas to all.

"You have to admit this is more fun than going home alone." His forehead wrinkled as he inspected the tree and stretched to straighten a branch, giving her another great view of his rear end. "You think I need to take a little more off the top? I want this tree to look amazing when we're done."

What she thought was that no amount of trimming was going to make the tree come anywhere near to how amazing his bottom was. Someone should stick him at the top of the tree and her views on Christmas might brighten more than a little. Definitely, she could get into unwrapping his package.

Urgh. What was wrong with her? Perhaps Riley had placed a spell on her beneath the mistletoe because she'd really like him to climb down that stepladder, take her in his arms and kiss her until her lungs were so deprived of oxygen she had to pull away just to keep from losing consciousness.

Then she wanted him to kiss her some more. More. More. More.

Crazy. She wanted to be kissed right now. And not because of some silly song coming over his surround-sound system about a kid seeing momma kissing Santa either. Riley's belly could never be compared to a bowl full of jelly and the dusky five o'clock shadow gracing the strong lines of his jaw were sexy, not fluffy white tufts that would tickle her face.

"Are you hanging mistletoe?" Oops. Had she really just asked that out loud? Who needed the cozy fire that he must have also turned on to keep the room temperature comfortable? Her face had to have just sped up global warming with a single embarrassing moment.

He glanced down at her, his grin positively lethal. "Would you like me to hang mistletoe, princess?"

How did any good girl in her right mind answer that?

"Um, no, I was just wondering if you were going to, not suggesting you do so, *snowflake*. I mean, if you were going to that would be okay, but if not…" Okay, time to zip her lips because she was rambling and just fanning the flames.

The dimple in his left cheek dug deeper. "You know, I'm a traditional kind of guy so I do have mistletoe. It's in that box over by the sofa if you want to dig it out."

Just to have an excuse to move away from his gaze, she went to the plastic storage container and searched through the labeled boxes inside. When she lifted the lid off the properly labeled one she wrinkled her nose. "You insist on a live tree but have plastic mistletoe?"

"I know. A travesty." He gave a faux devastated shrug. "We should go shopping tomorrow evening to buy me the real deal."

"I wasn't hinting for an invitation."

"I didn't think you were."

"I have better things to do."

"Than to enjoy the spirit of Christmas?" He gave her a horrified look. "What could be better than that?"

"Just about anything and everything."

"Don't you like Christmas?" Obviously he found the possibility that someone might not like Christmas so absurd he didn't wait for an answer, just climbed down the ladder to survey his handiwork.

"It's not my favorite holiday," she muttered under her breath, glad that at least for the moment she didn't have to stare up at his amazing butt.

Her answer caught his attention and he glanced at her. "Which holiday is your favorite, then?"

Not that she'd ever discussed her aversion to Christmas with anyone, but no one had ever asked her which holiday was her favorite. She thought for a moment.

"New Year's Day." She blinked at the man standing right in front of her.

"Why's that? You like making resolutions no one ever keeps?"

"And people think I'm cynical?" Smiling, she shook her head. "No."

Besides, she tended to keep the few New Year's resolutions she made each year. Somehow she'd bet Riley did his best to keep any resolutions he made too. He just seemed like that kind of guy.

"After New Year is when everyone takes all their Christmas decorations down and gets on with their real life, instead of wasting a month dreaming dreams about a man in a red suit bringing them their heart's desire."

"Ouch." He placed his hand over his heart and took a step back as if she'd struck him a vital blow. "You're a mean one, Miss Gr—"

She held up her hand and squinted at him. "Don't you call me names, snowflake." She tossed a loose piece of mistletoe at him, smiling when he easily caught it and blew her a kiss.

She puckered up and kissed the air. Electricity sizzled between them and she clung to their conversation to keep her mind away from just how much she wanted to feel his lips against hers for real. "Not liking this superficial holiday that's a bunch of marketing hype to get people to spend money that they don't have does not make me a bad person...or a green one."

His lips twitched, as if he knew what she was doing, as if his lips had a few wants of their own. "Agreed, but I'd really like to know why someone who's as sweet as you wouldn't like the most wonderful time of year."

"First off, whether or not Christmas is the most wonderful time of the year is a matter of opinion." Was he moving closer or was she imagining that the distance between them was shrinking? Oh, please, let the distance be shrinking because if he didn't kiss her soon, she might just bury herself in mistletoe and present herself to him. "Obviously," she continued, as if her heart wasn't pounding in her chest, as if every cell within her didn't leap toward him, "I am not of that opinion."

"Second?" He'd definitely moved closer. A lot closer. She could feel his body heat, could feel his breath brush across her lips, could smell his musky male scent that sent her senses into hyperdrive.

"Second..." she stared into his eyes, her lips parted, her pulse throbbing "...you don't know me well enough to know how sweet I may or may not be."

"I disagree." He covered her mouth with his, moved his lips in a caress that was teasing, tasting, erotic and sensual. Hot and demanding. Everything she'd just been longing for. Him. His kiss made her feel as if someone had strung lights on her and she twinkled from the inside out.

"Oh, yeah, you're sweet," he whispered against her lips when he pulled back. "Sweet as candy canes and gumdrops."

"Right," was all she could manage, because what she really wanted was to pull his mouth back to hers. Desperately she wanted another kiss, wanted him. That terrified her. "Let's get this tree decorated so I can go home."

After a brief pause, in which he studied her, Riley threw his head back in laughter. "You know, princess, if I didn't know any better, I'd think you like me even less than you profess to like Christmas."

"Good thing you know better, then, eh?" she retorted, handing him one of the new strings of lights. "Get to hanging or I'm out of here."

Because at the moment she was having a difficult time recalling all the reasons she shouldn't want him and needed not to trust in him.

"Yes, ma'am." With a wicked gleam in his eyes he reached for the mistletoe and went to hold it above her head. "I'll start with your favorite decoration."

"No!" But she ruined her denial by having to suppress a laugh. She pointed to the tree. "Decorate."

He gave an exaggerated sigh. "I didn't know you were such a slavedriver."

She gave him the sternest look she could muster when he looked so darned cute and remorseful with his mistletoe. "Like I said, there are a lot of things about me you don't know."

"Yet," he clarified, with what she was quickly realizing was his usual optimism. Or was stubbornness a better label? "Don't worry," he continued. "I plan to know everything there is to know about you, princess."

Lord, she hoped not. She'd come to Pensacola to escape people who knew everything there was to know about her.

"You'll be coming to me to find yourself," he added, his expression way too confident.

She hoped not on that too because she never wanted to let anyone that close ever again.

"Here, you save this for later." He tucked the loose piece of mistletoe she'd tossed at him into her scrub top pocket. "Any time you get the urge, you just wave that and I'll pucker up."

She rolled her eyes but couldn't keep her fingers away from the cheap plastic greenery in her pocket. "Like a red flag in front of a bull?"

He chuckled. "I hope I have a little more finesse than that." His brow furrowed in mock concern. "I do have more finesse than a stampeding cow, right?"

She gave a little shrug. "Maybe."

His brow rose.

"Okay," she confessed. "A little."

"I'll settle for that for now, but later we'll renegotiate your thoughts about my finesse."

If that meant he planned to kiss her again, she should find a reason to leave, but instead she just smiled and secretly hoped that was precisely what he meant.

Prior to placing the lights on the tree, they plugged the strands in to make sure each bulb lit up. Each one shone a brilliant color, sparkling against the tiled flooring. Then she held the lights while he went back up the stepladder. They worked together to string them around the tree, starting at top and working their way down.

Every time she started to enjoy herself a little too much, she reined herself in because he made her feel a little too happy, a little too comfy, and that could only lead to heartache, right? She couldn't deal with more heartache so it was much better to keep her defenses high.

Telling herself she really did not like the woodsy scent filling her nostrils and that she'd probably have a rash on her hands from handling the branches, Trinity frowned. "Why do you have such a big tree?"

He waggled his brows, covering the last of the branches with lights. "You know what they say about men with big Christmas trees."

The man was a certifiable nut. She must be too because she almost giggled. So much for her defenses. "They have big trees to compensate for their wee little...minds?"

He gave her a scolding look. "I could show you my wee little mind and put that theory to rest."

"You wish," she teased, before thinking better of it.

He reached for the snap at his waist.

"Fine." She didn't bother suppressing her eye-roll but tried really hard to keep her blush in check. "Please, tell me, oh great ginormous tree owner, why is your tree so big?"

His eyes sparkled and his grin almost knocked her off her feet. "The bigger the tree, the better to light up her world."

"Her?" He hadn't brought anyone with him to the hospital Christmas party, had spent the evening with her, had spent the night afterwards in her bed and flirted outrageously with her. He'd better not have a "her".

"Your world?" he corrected, looking sheepish.

"I don't need your compensatory huge tree lighting up my world. My world is just fine the way it is."

Even as she made the bold claim, she wondered if perhaps she did because when he clicked a button and his tree sparkled to life, she had to admit, something inside her felt better. Warmer.

Lighter.

As if the button had turned on something inside her too that had been stuck in hibernation.

"Wow," she gasped, unable to quash her surprise. "I have to admit, that's beautiful."

Exactly, Riley thought, but he wasn't looking at the tree. He couldn't drag his eyes away from Trinity.

She was beautiful.

He wanted to light up her world, to see a permanent sparkle in her eyes and a smile on her lips.

Too bad he didn't have a remote control that he could click and turn her on.

To turn her on in more ways than one.

Because he was turned on.

Had been from the moment he'd first noticed her at the Christmas party. Something about her got under his skin and made his body go haywire. Big time. Was it just that instead of chasing him, like most women did, she seemed intent on keeping him at arm's length?

"Just wait until you see it after we've finished decorating," he promised. "My tree, which I refuse to label as compensatory and would still be more than happy to set the record straight once and for all, will steal your breath, guaranteed."

"I…" She glanced away then her lips tightened. "I seriously doubt that, but I do like the lights." She wasn't going to touch his offer apparently. Not that he'd really expected her to. "Let's hurry and finish."

"So you can leave?"

She met his gaze, her lips twitching lightly, letting him know she was fighting back a smile. "So I can have some of that dessert you promised but have totally failed to deliver."

"Touché." He laughed.

Yes, he really liked this woman, even if she professed not to like his favorite holiday. There had to be more to her claim than just a dislike of Christmas.

A more that he wanted to know every detail of so he could prove her wrong and show her the magic of the holidays.

CHAPTER FIVE

TRINITY DIDN'T LIKE Christmas at all and doubted she ever would. But when they'd finished decorating, she did think that Riley's Christmas tree was beautiful. Magical even.

Plus, she had concluded that she did like the woodsy pine smell filling his living room. Why had she practically gagged on the scent for the past couple of years, comparing the outdoorsy aroma to spruce-scented household cleaner?

Because she didn't like this holiday, she reminded herself.

From childhood this holiday had only ever held bad memories. Nothing good had ever come out of Christmas. Not for her.

She'd do well to remember that.

Riley's constant smiles and holiday good cheer made her forget that she didn't like a single thing about the season. Still, she was doing something to help someone who had helped her. Someone she genuinely liked and who hadn't taken advantage of her.

"Thank you."

"For?" he asked, studying her way too intently for her comfort.

She wanted to squirm, like a kid sitting on Santa's lap. "Last night."

"Nothing happened last night for you to owe me any thanks for."

Was that how he saw the night?

"Had something happened," she admitted, "I wouldn't have been thanking you."

"You might have," he teased, but when she didn't smile, he relented. "For the record, I prefer my bed partners to be sober and just as into me as I am into them. Whether or not we were going to have sex last night was never an issue."

"I wasn't into you?" That she had a hard time imagining because the man made her burn from head to toe. Even now she wanted to rip his clothes off him and lick him all over. She squeezed her eyes shut, trying to clear the image of her doing just that.

He shrugged. "We've already established that you drank a little too much."

"Did I want you?" she said, more insistently. What was she saying? Of course she'd wanted him. She still wanted him.

"You said you did."

"Oh." A vague memory of her telling him he could do whatever he wanted so long as he didn't leave her ran through her mind. Fire spread across her cheeks. She had made a complete and utter fool of herself. "I'm sorry." She turned to go, wishing her car was in his drive so she really could escape.

"I'm not." He turned her to face him. "I wanted you, Trinity. I'm not ashamed to say so."

She blushed and he grinned.

"I wasn't inebriated, except by your smile."

"I've said it before but it bears repeating, you're smooth with the lines, Riley."

"No lines," he said. "Just the truth."

"Right."

"Seriously."

"Seriously, I want that dessert now." Anything to get away from this conversation.

"Chicken," he accused, apparently reading her well enough to know exactly what she was doing.

"Bok bok, Mr. Big Tree," she replied, wondering at her sparring back and forth with him verbally when really she should be embarrassed at her out-of-character behavior.

His laugh made her feel warm inside.

"Like I said, fun girl."

"Like I said, give me dessert."

Trinity had expected Riley to insist on coming into her apartment when he'd followed her home, but he didn't. He walked her to her door, kissed her forehead, saw her inside, then left without setting foot into her place.

Go figure.

Staring at the closed door, she wanted to open it, to yell to him that he could have at least kissed her goodnight properly.

'Meow.' Casper brushed up against her leg, reminding Trinity that she'd like to be fed.

"I know. I know. I rushed off this morning without paying you much attention." She glanced down at the solid white cat that she'd rescued from an animal shelter when she had been nothing more than a tiny pitiful-looking kitten.

Casper mewed again, staying practically beneath her

feet as she walked towards her small pantry to get a can of cat food. She opened the can, put the contents into Casper's dish and watched the cat dive in with gusto.

"You'd think you were starved," she teased. "But I am fully aware that Riley fed you this morning while I threw on my scrubs."

That he'd been thoughtful enough to do so had impressed her, even if she hadn't made a big deal of him having done so. The man was thoughtful all the way round. He was just a little too good to be true.

Well, all except for the not having kissed her goodnight part. That he could use some work on.

Or maybe it was her sanity that could use some work, because she shouldn't want him to kiss her. She didn't want a relationship, didn't want to set herself up for another fall, like the one Chase had delivered.

"I know you aren't starved," she informed the cat.

Casper's blue eyes cut to her for a brief second as if to say, So what?

Trinity laughed then jumped when her phone rang. She glanced at the number. It wasn't one she was familiar with, but she knew who the caller was as sure as she lived and breathed. Should she answer?

Could she not?

"Did you forget something?" she said by way of greeting, because "Hello" seemed all wrong when he had just left.

"Apparently." He sounded confused, frustrated. "I'm standing outside your front door."

Trinity's stomach flip-flopped. Had he ever left? Or had he just come back? Did it matter?

"The usual protocol when standing outside someone's door is to knock, not phone." Her heart pounding in anticipation of whatever was to come, she headed towards the front door.

"I didn't knock because I don't want to come in."

Her hand paused in the process of reaching for the doorknob. "You don't?"

Her stomach knotted. Was he playing some sick game with her? Teasing her? Toying with her emotions?

"I do, but...Trinity, tell me to go home."

If this was his idea of a game, it was cruel and twisted. She wasn't amused.

"Go home," she ordered, and meant it. She'd been hurt enough in the past. She wouldn't let someone sour her future. Not even someone who seemed as wonderful as Riley.

Then again, most of the time when something seemed too good to be true, it really was. So why was she still on the line, waiting for him to say something? Hoping he'd say something. Something brilliant and wonderful that would make her smile instead of feeling as if her eyes were about to spring a leak.

A low laugh sounded in her ears. "That was way too easy for you, princess."

"You have no idea," she muttered, wondering at the silence that followed. She wanted to tear the door off its hinges and drag him inside her apartment and demand he explain himself.

Instead, she leaned her forehead against the cold metal doorframe, wishing she could see through it to the other side, wishing she knew what he was thinking, why he was standing outside her door when she was inside, why he'd called her instead of knocking.

Why was he there at all?

Why wasn't she hanging up?

Urgh. Her head hurt with all the questions plaguing her mind.

"If I knocked, would you let me in, princess?" His voice was barely above a whisper but she heard just fine.

Her hands shook. "I guess you'll have to knock to know the answer to that question, won't you, snowflake?"

Taking a deep breath, he laughed again. "If you had any idea how much I want to rip through this door because I know you're standing just the other side..." He paused, and she'd swear she felt his forehead bump against the door. Was he trying to knock some sense into his head? How was it he kept putting her thoughts into words that came from his mouth?

"As much as I want you," he admitted, "what I want more than anything is to not mess this up."

"Knocking on my door would mess this up?" What was "this", she wanted to ask, but held her tongue. She doubted he knew any more than she did. That he admitted there was a "this" was monumental, had her brain undoing every wall she'd just attempted to erect between them. Didn't he know he should leave those walls alone? She needed them.

"It might. What if you didn't open the door?"

He had a point.

"True, but what if I did?"

Or would that be messing things up even worse?

Riley ground his forehead against the cold, hard metal of Trinity's apartment door and prayed for the knowledge to know the right thing to do.

He wanted to knock.

Whether she would admit to it or not, she wanted him to knock. He could hear it in her voice.

Every instinct warned he shouldn't, that, despite their mutual desire for one another, she wasn't ready to consummate that desire. Not really.

As much as he hated listening to that voice of reason, he trusted his instincts more than the body part that had him wanting to he-man his way into her apartment.

To do that would only satisfy him in the short term and although he had no clue exactly what he wanted with Trinity, he knew that one night would not be enough. If he rushed, she might shut him out for ever. Despite the tough front she attempted to put on, she was vulnerable in ways that made him want to fight every dragon that had ever taken a swipe at her. Although he didn't understand or like how protective he felt about her, he refused to be yet another dragon for her to fend off, even if a well-intentioned one.

"We both know you shouldn't open your door to me. Not tonight." He straightened from the door before he gave in to temptation.

"Then why did you call?" She sounded irked, which pleased him because it meant she wasn't immune to the chemistry between them. That he wasn't wrong.

"Why call?" He loved her logic and her sass. Despite the rebellious throb in his body, he couldn't help but smile. "To hear your voice. For you to tell me I'm crazy."

"You're crazy," she replied, without hesitation.

"About you," he admitted, knowing it was true, that she was different from any woman he'd ever known, and not just because she didn't fall at his feet.

Which was why he'd leave, and smile while doing so. Yeah, he'd like to be on the other side of her door but there was no rush. He'd take his time, woo her, have her begging for more, and then give her more for however long the sparks between them flew.

"You don't even know me," she insisted, much as she'd done previously.

"A problem I intend to remedy."

But not tonight.

Forehead against the door, Trinity held her breath. Surely, any second now he'd knock. He had to knock, right?

He was there.

Just on the other side of her door, teasing her. No, not teasing really. More of a temptation to reach out and take what she reluctantly admitted she wanted.

He did tempt her. Like fresh-baked cookies tempted a starving dieter.

She wanted a bite.

A big bite.

Before she could have biter's remorse, she undid the chain, undid the deadbolt and flung the door open.

"Riley?"

"Hmm?" His response buzzed in her ear.

"Where are you?" Stunned, she glanced down the hallway.

The empty hallway.

"My car."

His car?

He'd left?

Her heart sank.

"You were never really on the other side of my door?"

She might kill him. He'd gotten her all worked up for nothing, had...

"I was there."

Frowning, fighting disappointment she didn't quite understand and definitely didn't want, she went back into her apartment. She should hang up now, before she incriminated herself.

Why was she surprised? Disappointed? She should be glad he'd left, that he'd had reason when she'd temporarily lost her mind. Her stomach knotted and her eyes watered. Great.

Why was she not telling him where to go and turning off her phone?

"Trinity?"

"Yes?" She slumped back against the door, fighting a sniffle. Was he seriously whistling? She might just throw her phone at him for real.

"I like you."

Were they in grammar school or what?

Eyes squeezed closed, she sighed. "So you keep saying, but at the moment, Riley Williams, I don't like you one bit."

He surprised her by bursting into laughter. "There's my funny girl."

"Are you dating Dr. Williams?"

Putting her stethoscope into her scrub pocket, Trinity spun around to look at her coworker. Karen Mathis, Trinity's favorite coworker by far—usually—grinned at her and waited with an expectant look that said she wasn't going to be easily distracted.

"Why would you ask me that?"

"I saw you at the Christmas party," Karen pointed out. "I'd been looking for you because I knew you didn't know many people yet and I was going to have you join the group I was with. I didn't spot you until you were all cozied up with the only cardiologist on staff who makes women's hearts beat faster with just a flash of his smile."

Trinity's heart was beating pretty fast without the benefit of one of his smiles. "We just danced. It wasn't a big deal."

"And sang together," Karen reminded her. "Plus, I hear you arrived at work with him yesterday morning when you both got called in. You rode home with him yesterday at the end of your shift. Despite many females' valiant efforts, I don't know of him ever dating anyone who works here. This all sounds like a big deal to me. So, are you two an item or what?"

Inwardly, Trinity cringed. The hospital gossip mill had sure been busy. How did she answer a question she didn't know the answer to? Because saying he liked her just sounded a bit second grade to her. She didn't really know what they were other than that she liked him too.

"Did you also hear that she's going to eat with me after work tonight?"

Both women turned at the newcomer to their conversation.

"Dr. Williams." Karen's cheeks flushed almost as bright as Trinity imagined hers were.

"Riley," she gasped, her eyes devouring the man before her, searching his eyes for some trace of the man who'd spent hours on the phone with her the night before. Hours and hours. He'd blown her away. They'd talked long into the night without awkwardness or long bouts of weird silence. The man was way too easy to talk to. "Anyone ever tell you it isn't polite to eavesdrop?"

She almost called him "snowflake" but caught

herself just in time. Yeah, that would have had some tongues wagging all over the cardiac unit.

"Never. Most people like having conversations with me." He waggled his brows, his eyes not leaving Trinity's. The twinkle there said everything. That he knew what she was thinking, was thinking the same thing himself. "Good morning, ladies."

Trinity mumbled a good morning, glancing away because all she could think was that this was the man with whom she'd fallen asleep while on the phone with him the night before.

He'd stayed on the phone with her because he'd said he really did want to get to know her without the physical getting in the way. Honestly, she just didn't know what to think about him. He was unlike any many she'd ever met.

Chase sure hadn't worried about the physical getting in the way.

Sex had gotten in the way of their relationship.

Big time.

Not because they'd rushed into a physical relationship. They hadn't, despite Chase's constant pressure to do so. Perhaps she should have held out longer. When she'd finally given in, it had been the beginning of the end. She'd flopped in bed.

Chase had had no qualms announcing that juicy little tidbit to the world.

So a man who put emphasis on getting to know her rather than on her bedroom performance was good. Raised her odds of success, right? Or just set up her expectations to where her failure would sting all the more?

"Trinity?" Riley interrupted her thoughts. "We *are* going to eat after work today?"

She blinked, thinking him too good looking for his own good. He was so used to getting his own way that she almost said no just to be difficult. But that wasn't any way to start a relationship. Or to maintain one.

A relationship. Was that what they were doing? What she wanted?

"Yes," she agreed, knowing she wasn't going to deprive herself of spending the evening with him, even if she still didn't trust him. "Just as long as we don't do anything Christmassy."

For answer, he just grinned. "Would I ever ask you to do that?"

"Never." Trinity couldn't keep a smile from curving her lips. She tried. Really, she did. After all, she had sworn off men, but there was something about Riley that couldn't be ignored. Okay, so everything about him refused to be ignored.

Karen stared back and forth between them. "So the gossip is true?"

Trinity blushed.

Riley grinned. "If they're saying that I'm pursuing the hottest nurse at Pensacola Memorial then, yeah, it's true."

Had he really just said that? Trinity's face caught fire and her mouth dropped. Chase had always been so private, not wanting anyone to know how much he cared about her, saying that with them both working for the hospital they should keep their relationship on the quiet. Ha, he'd sure blown that at the end.

Then again, had he really cared about her at all? She'd certainly thought so. They'd dated for nine months. She'd thought she was going to get an engagement ring for Christmas. Instead, she'd gotten a horrendous public humiliation and a reminder about why she disliked the holiday so much. Or perhaps it was Christmas that disliked her. Maybe she should ask Riley for a rain check until New Year.

Karen smiled. "I'll be sure to let everyone know you're off the market, Dr. Williams."

"I didn't know I was ever on the market. But you do that. My free time is definitely going to be occupied by this little lady so long as she'll let me hang around." Riley winked and nodded towards the cardiac care patient rooms. "How's Mr. Ryker this morning? Holding his own?"

Still not quite believing how he'd just essentially given Karen permission to tell everyone that he belonged to her, Trinity shook her head in wonder.

Take that, Christmas party trio who'd called her "tonight's lucky pick".

She was this week's lucky pick.

Or something like that.

Then again, she had to wonder just what he had to gain by hanging out with her. Why he'd want to. Ultimately, how much did they have in common? Was he so used to women chasing him that he had to dazzle her so she'd follow suit?

Sure, she'd enjoyed talking to him into the wee hours, but everything was different when you were bone tired, right?

Still, she'd be lying if she said she hadn't enjoyed spending time with him the evening before, despite what he'd had her doing. She'd definitely be fibbing if she said she hadn't derived deep pleasure from falling asleep to the sound of his voice, to his breathing on the other end of the phone, to him asking her thoughts and dreams.

No one had ever asked her those things.

"Oxygen sats are staying at 97-98%, but he's still on two liters per minute," she told him, referring to the patient she'd just finished checking prior to Karen's inquisition. "Cardiac monitoring is normal. His vitals are stable. Ins and outs are normal. A physical therapist had him up walking not long ago."

"That's what I like to hear."

It's what she liked to report. No nurse wanted to deliver bad news regarding a patient.

"Come round with me?"

He was her superior so of course she'd go round with him if that's what he wanted. Based on the past couple days, she'd do a lot of things with him if that's what he wanted. If he could get her to decorate a Christmas tree, she was pretty much at his will to command.

Lord, she hoped that wasn't really so.

"Y'all have fun and don't do anything that will get Mr. Ryker's heart racing," Karen teased, looking quite pleased at Riley's admission.

He laughed and Trinity didn't say a word. Honestly, as impressed as she was at Riley not caring who knew he was interested in her, she hated the thought that she was the focus of hospital gossip. Even if it was positive gossip regarding her and Riley, because all good things came to an end and then what? She'd once again be poor pitiful Trinity who'd been dumped, because realistically she acknowledged that he'd be the one to end their relationship.

Would he humiliate her publicly, the way Chase had?

Of course, to give him credit, Chase had been drinking too much. Would he have otherwise announced her shortcomings so cruelly at their hospital Christmas party? Probably not, but once done he'd been unable to take back his words, couldn't stop the teasing that had ensued at Trinity's expense. Why had she stayed in Memphis so long after that horrible Christmas? Had she purposely been punishing herself for being so stupid as to put her hopes in a man? At least she hadn't started drinking, the way her mother had after being deserted by Trinity's father.

She should have removed herself from the situation much sooner. She hadn't wanted to run but, really, after her mother's death she'd had no ties. She should have left. Next time she'd know.

Next time?

Was she already planning for the demise of any relationship between her and Riley? Whatever that relationship might be. She really didn't have a clue what he wanted from her.

If he'd just wanted sex, wouldn't he have knocked the night before instead of talking to her into the wee morning hours?

Riley tapped on the patient's door then entered the private cardiac room. "Good morning, Mr. Ryker."

The man stretched out in his bed smiled at Riley and then at Trinity. A clear tube ran around his face with a nasal cannula delivering oxygen. Multiple wires and leads were attached at various points to his body.

"Your nurse tells me that you're ready to dance a jig and you want to blow this joint as soon as possible. That so?"

Not her exact words.

"If it would get me home earlier, I'd dance a jig or

two," the heavy set man admitted, raising the head of his bed and scooting up, wincing a little as he did so. "Other than the pain in my chest and leg from being cut open, I feel great."

"If all goes well today, I'll release you to go home tomorrow morning and see you back in the office in a week or so."

The man's wife, who'd been sitting quietly in a chair next to his hospital bed, got wide-eyed. "You're going to let him go home that soon? Is that safe?"

"If everything goes as expected today, yes, I am. It's safe for him to go home. Actually, the sooner I can get him home, the less risk there is of secondary infections such as a resistant strain of staph or C. diff."

"Oh," the woman blanched and she pushed a heavy-framed pair of glasses up the bridge of her nose. "What if something else happens? I won't know how to take care of him."

"If it's a problem, we can have a home health agency come out and dress his chest wounds and the surgical site on his leg. But, honestly, he should be fine as long as he doesn't overdo it."

The woman's relief was evident.

"But the first thing we have to do is get you through today." Riley placed his stethoscope on the man's chest, moving the diaphragm from spot to spot to listen to the man's heart sounds.

"Can you tell if the bypass is taking, based on what you hear?" the man asked, looking concerned. "I keep wondering what I'd do if my heart rejected the graft."

"That's unlikely to happen as it's your own tissue. But no worries, we'll take another look at the blood flow via an echocardiogram to make sure everything is working properly. You're in good hands."

Trinity wouldn't argue with Riley's claim. He did have good hands. Expert hands that worked magic with hearts.

Which, of course, made her wonder about what those hands were going to do to her heart.

Or should she even worry about that since Chase had tattered it to shreds and despite her move she knew there were only broken pieces where once a strong heart used to beat?

Maybe she was immune to Riley hurting her because she didn't have a heart left to be broken.

Somehow she doubted that because already she knew she'd miss him terribly if he left her life.

That scared her more than she cared to admit. Maybe she should run while she still could.

Only could she, even if she wanted to?

CHAPTER SIX

"This isn't dinner," Trinity pointed out when Riley pulled into the crowded mall parking lot that evening. Although he looked handsome in khakis and a polo and was in way too good a mood to have worked all day, she was still in her scrubs, hungry, tired and really didn't want to fight the crowds. She'd told him she'd have dinner with him, so dinner they would have.

Somehow she hadn't envisioned him taking her to a shopping center for a slice of pizza or Chinese. Then again, she knew next to nothing about his eating habits and they had eaten sandwiches the night before.

"True," Riley admitted, not looking one bit guilty as he parked the car in a just-vacated parking spot.

One more thing to not like about Christmas. Everywhere was packed. Parking lots, shops, streets. It was as if every person came out of hibernation and crowded every public place, searching for that great deal on the perfect gift that they'd spend money they didn't really have to spend. Trinity would much rather be at home with a good book and Casper curled up in her lap than dealing with all the holiday hoopla.

Her car door opened and she glanced up at the man

waiting for her to get out of the car. Really? She'd rather be with her cat than with this gorgeous man?

Okay, so not really. But hanging with Casper would be a lot easier on her emotions in the long run.

Please, don't hurt me, she silently pleaded. All day she'd questioned why he'd taken an interest in her when there were so many women out there who would gladly kiss his rear end and had to be more suitable than her. She was just Trinity Warren from the wrong side of the tracks, so to speak. He was a cardiac surgeon who'd obviously led a privileged life. They couldn't be more different.

"Come on, princess." A big smile on his face, he motioned for her to get out of the car. "We're just going to do a little shopping before we eat."

What? He wanted her to go in there and face the shopping frenzy? Had he lost his mind?

"I don't think so. You didn't mention anything about shopping."

"Didn't I?" He pretended to look repentant. "Must have slipped my mind." He took her hand and laced their fingers together. "No worries, princess. I promise to feed you, too."

As if skipping a meal or two would hurt her.

Still, the last thing she wanted was to go into a mall all decked out with Christmas decorations and sales. Maybe she really was a Scrooge.

"I don't like shopping." Had she sounded petulant? It hadn't been her intent, but she felt like digging her heels in and refusing to budge. Seriously, the man did not have to have his way on everything.

"Every woman likes to shop."

She snorted. How stereotypically male!

"Shows how much you know about women," she countered, chin high at his arrogant comment.

He stopped walking and gawked at her. "How can you not like shopping? Especially at this time of year? Every store is a smorgasbord of treats just waiting to make someone happy."

Her stomach roiled. "It's especially at this time of year I don't like shopping and my guess is that that smorgasbord of treats causes more problems than happiness. Someone has to pay for all that stuff bought that no one really needed to begin with."

Wow. She sounded a lot like her mother.

Which she really didn't want because, God rest her soul, Trinity didn't want any similarity between herself and the woman who'd given birth to her. Still, facts were facts. People went crazy at Christmas.

"Bah, humbug."

"Make fun of me all you like, but I prefer if we eat and then you take me home before you do your shopping." If his lower lip stuck out any further she'd swear he was pouting. "Or you can just take me home now and you can come back and do your shopping. We can do dinner some other time."

"We're not doing my shopping and no way am I taking you home without feeding you first."

This time she was the one who stopped walking. She stared at him as if he was making no sense. Actually, he wasn't making any sense.

"Whose shopping are we doing?"

"Yours."

Her face squished and her nose curled in disgust. "Mine?"

He nodded, tweaking her nose to unfurrow the wrinkles.

"I don't need to do any shopping." Her needs were simple and she wasn't running low on anything. Who would she buy something for? She barely knew anyone in Pensacola and as much as she liked Karen, she wasn't sure they were at a buy-each-other-Christmas-gifts point in their friendship. Although she did like the woman and Karen had seemed happy for her regarding Riley's interest, so maybe... Trinity usually just ordered a few gift cards online to have on hand in case she needed a quick gift. Last year she'd used most of them herself come January because she just hadn't had anyone to give them to.

"Sure you do," Riley countered with so much confidence that her insides heated a little.

She blew out a frustrated sigh. "Riley, I don't like it when you assume things about me."

A serious expression slid over his face. "Noted. I don't mean to railroad you into doing something you don't want to do, princess. But I also feel it my personal responsibility to get you into the Christmas spirit."

His personal responsibility? Poor guy. He had no clue what he was in for.

"Good luck with that."

"Thanks."

She shook her head, not surprised her sarcasm had fallen short. Riley only seemed to see the positive, regardless of what she did or said.

Still, Christmas was pushing it. Why couldn't they have met at a Halloween party? Or, better yet, a New Year party? Anything but Christmas because taking away the fact that he was a gorgeous doctor and she was just her, the fact they'd met at a Christmas party spelled doom from the start.

So far as she was concerned, nothing good had ever come out of Christmas.

But the sooner they got this shopping ordeal over with the sooner they could eat and the sooner she could go home and over-analyze the past few days yet again. "What am I shopping for?"

"It's less than two weeks until Christmas Day and you don't have a single decoration up or a single wrapped present in your apartment."

That was a problem why? Her apartment was the one place she could escape from all the holiday craziness.

"I hate to burst your bubble, Riley, but most single people without kids don't go all out with decorations and presents. They have better things to do with their time than decorating for themselves."

Like take out the trash and give the cat a bath. Important things like those.

He shook his head in mock disappointment, his eyes twinkling. "I bet you were one of those kids who never believed in Santa and took joy in telling other kids that he wasn't real."

Although she doubted he'd meant his comment to hurt, she felt a sharp sting in her chest and a defensive shield popped up. "I never told other kids Santa wasn't real."

He stared at her incredulously. "But you never believed in Santa? In the magic of Christmas? Not even as a kid?"

Swallowing the lump in her throat at memories she didn't want rising to the surface, she shook her head.

"Then who did you think climbed down your chimney and left all the Christmas morning goodies? The tooth fairy?"

She didn't think anything. Not about the tooth fairy or Santa. Or the Easter bunny or any other mythical creature who was supposed to do something good for her. Why would she?

"Apparently your Christmas mornings were very different from mine." At her house Christmas had just been another day. No big deal. Actually, if she'd made the mistake of mentioning the holidays, Christmas morning had been worse than other days because her mother would go into a bigger than normal rant. New Year had never been able to get there soon enough.

"Were you so naughty that Santa didn't visit?" His tone was teasing, but Trinity had to look away because she'd swear something had blown into her eyes. Probably a bit of fake snow off the ginormous tree gracing the entryway of the shopping mall.

Stupid tree. Stupid fake snow. Stupid shopping trip. Stupid her for coming here and dredging up all these memories.

She was not going to let him see her cry, had learned long ago to hide her pain. Most of the time, at any rate. So she slid her game face on, the same one she'd worn year after year.

"Apparently so, because he never did."

Riley stared at Trinity, trying to decide if she was joking. The pale undertones to her skin and tight set to her mouth before she'd turned away from him said she wasn't but that she would just as soon he thought she was.

He'd really stuck his foot in his mouth on this one. He'd been teasing her, wanting to make her smile, wanting to make her reveal more about herself, and she had. But he felt awful. Surely, she was over-exaggerating?

"Not even once?"

Her eyes downcast and expression somber, she shrugged. "It's not a big deal, Riley. We've been through this already. Christmas is just a commercial gimmick to make people spend money. I didn't need Santa bringing me presents. Not then or now."

The lift of her chin declared she didn't need anything and dared anyone to claim she did. Was that what she really believed? If so, shame on her parents.

"Didn't your parents believe in Christmas? In the joy of giving?" He couldn't imagine his own parents not making a big deal out of the holidays. It was the one and only time of the year his father took time away from work. His mother had barely been able to wait to get her house decorated. Pretty much the minute she had removed the remains of the turkey from the table at Thanksgiving, she'd have him and his brothers start carrying down precisely labeled totes of decorations. Despite whining, those times were some of his best memories.

Although he hadn't given it much conscious thought, he was carrying on in her footsteps right down to how he stored his Christmas goodies.

"Oh, my mother believed in the joy of giving all year long." But the way Trinity said the words conveyed a very different message from the one Riley had meant.

Poor Trinity, not having similar holiday traditions. As crazy as his family was, his Christmas memories were all good ones, except for those first few following his father's death when his mother had seemed lost and forlorn. Riley had vowed to give her back her Christmas mojo and he had. Their shopping and decorating spree the previous week was proof enough of that.

Trinity rubbed her hand across her forehead, sucked in a breath and stared into an electronics store window as if their display was the most fascinating thing she'd ever seen. For a brief moment he thought her eyes watered, but not a single tear fell so he might have been wrong.

But he doubted it.

"What about your father?"

She gave a low laugh. "I have no clue about my father's thoughts on Christmas, or anything else for that matter. He left before I was born."

That he could relate to on some levels, because although his father had lived in the same house he'd rarely been home. Except at Christmas.

He'd wanted to know more about Trinity and her comments had revealed more than any other statement that she'd ever made. Yet all it had really done was to pose more questions. Questions that he didn't think walking in a shopping mall was the right time to ask. But someday he wanted to tear down the walls she hid behind.

"Well, Trinity Warren, this is your lucky year, because this Christmas is going to be your best ever." He squeezed her hand, knowing if he'd brought joy back to his mother's holidays he could do so to Trinity's too. "I promise."

"It's really not a big deal." But the no big deal had her voice choking a little beyond what she was able to hide. Maybe her eyes really had watered.

"Christmas is just another day," she continued, protesting a little too much perhaps. "I usually volunteer to work. I really don't mind and really don't need a 'best ever' Christmas."

In years past, he'd volunteered to work as well so that others with children could be at home with their loved ones. He imagined he'd do the same this Christmas Day, too. His family all understood that he could be called away from celebrations at any time, but fortunately he'd always been at the family get-together for at least most of the day.

He loved the craziness of his family under one roof, of kids running around everywhere, shaking packages, wanting to know what Uncle Riley had bought them this year, and his mother warning that he'd better not have bought them anything that was going to cause a ruckus in her house. And, of course, he always did.

"My mom cooks a big Christmas lunch. My whole family goes. And I do mean the whole family. There's a bunch of us—aunts, uncles, my mother, two brothers and two sisters, and more nieces and nephews than I can count these days." He smiled at the thought of his family. "It's a bit of mayhem, but in a good way. Maybe you'd like to go with me?"

Her gaze cut to his and a panicky look shone in her eyes. "Why?"

Why? Good question because Trinity going with him would raise all kinds of questions and expectations in his family's minds. He'd never brought a woman home for the holidays.

"Because I'd like to take you with me." Despite whatever teasing and questions her presence triggered, he knew he'd never spoken truer words. "I want you to spend Christmas Day with me, to be there with me and my family, to see what Christmas is really like."

Because no way could she go with him and not be enchanted with the holidays.

Her eyes definitely a little misty, she sucked in a deep breath. "Like I said, I'll probably be working, so I shouldn't make any plans. Thanks, though."

That was a cop-out if he'd ever heard one. Why was she being so stubborn when he was offering to include her in his life? Something past girlfriends had begged for. He was offering to take Trinity to his most important family get-together, one he cherished and had never risked an outsider disrupting, and she was tossing it back in his face?

"But if you're not working, you'll go?" He resented having to push when she should be happy to be invited, but he wasn't going to let her be vague with her answer. She'd wiggle out of going if he let her.

"I'll be working."

He arched his brow. If having to work was all that stood in the way of her going with him, he'd find a way to get someone else to work in her stead. Even if it meant slipping someone a nice fat Christmas bonus out of his own pocket. He wanted Trinity with him and, as crazy as it was, he'd do almost anything to ensure she was. She needed to experience the magic of Christmas and what better way than with his family?

"Fine." She relented at his look.

He could tell she was only agreeing because she didn't think that whether or not she'd be working was an issue. She planned to work, would probably beg to work. A spark of annoyance flashed through him. Surely she didn't think he'd let her get away with that?

"If I'm not working, I'll go with you to Christmas dinner with your family." She gave him a stern look.

"But the next time you ask me out to dinner, there had better actually be food involved rather than shopping because, in case you couldn't tell by looking at me, I'm not one of those girls who skips meals."

He threw his head back in laughter. "Funny girl. You're perfect just as you are, princess, and should never skip meals. No worries. I will feed you. Right after we buy your decorations."

CHAPTER SEVEN

THE LAST THING Trinity wanted in her apartment was Christmas decorations. She certainly didn't want to waste her hard-earned money on glittery, glowing fake trees and wreaths and garlands. Just having to walk through the aisles of ornaments and bows made her skin crawl.

She fought the urge to throw her hands into the air and run out of the store. This was pure torture.

Telling Riley the truth about her childhood had been torture. Why had she done so?

She'd never told anyone. Not even Chase. She'd not wanted to see the look of pity in his eyes, hadn't wanted anyone's pity. She was doing just fine, had a good life overall. She didn't need some man coming along and stirring up all kinds of childhood hang-ups to go along with the new ones Chase had hand-delivered two years ago.

She hadn't liked the sympathy in Riley's eyes. She didn't need his sympathy. She hadn't needed him to invite her to spend Christmas with his family out of pity.

"What about this?" Riley asked, pointing out a box of red glass balls. He'd already pointed out more than two dozen decorations, all of which she'd turned down.

She could tell he was losing patience with her. Good. Hopefully, he'd soon take the hint that she really didn't want to be doing this. Maybe she could fake a stomach growl to speed things along. She willed her stomach to let loose with a loud rumble, but didn't even manage a tiny one.

Great, the one time she wanted loud body noises around a hot guy and she couldn't even force one out. It figured.

Barely glancing at what he held, she shook her head. "No, thank you. Not interested. Besides, I really don't need any decorations. Just dinner."

"I've never met anyone who needs decorations more than you." His frustration was obvious and rubbed her wrong.

"I think I'm offended by that comment." She hadn't asked him to take her shopping, had only agreed to dinner, not a stroll down holiday horror lane.

He raked his fingers through his hair, glanced around the aisle then faced her. "I didn't mean it in a bad way."

"Because there's a good way to say someone needs plastic garland, fake glass balls and gaudy red velvet bows?"

"Precisely." Obviously having whipped his frustration into control, he grinned and held up a box of horrid cheap plastic candy canes for her inspection. "What about these? Awesome, right?"

Hoping he'd take the hint, Trinity didn't hide her boredom, just yawned. "If I pretended that my blood sugar was bottoming out, could we go and eat? Please?"

His gaze narrowed suspiciously. "Is your sugar dropping?"

She grimaced then shook her head. "No, but I could fake it."

He touched her chin, tilted her face towards him. "As long as I have breath in my body, I don't ever want you faking anything. I don't want you to even have need of faking anything." His lips twitched. "And I do mean *anything*."

His fingers burned her skin, singeing her flesh with the feel of him. She stepped back before she did something stupid. Like say she wanted to buy mistletoe. Bunches and bunches of mistletoe. Barrels of it.

"Okay, deal," she agreed, hoping he didn't see how his touch had made her pulse race and her breath catch. "Feed me, so I don't have to fake interest in shopping."

He shook his head in obvious displeasure. "If you really want to go, we'll go, but I'm disappointed that we didn't find a single thing you wanted."

She wanted him to touch her again, and in more places than just her chin. Did that count? It should because it was a really big want.

Then she saw it.

At the end of the aisle on a platform. A ten-and-a–half-foot blue spruce fake tree decorated with snow-flakes and angels and silver ribbon that twined back and forth between the branches. A toy train set was wound around the base and a few packages assured hidden delights but were probably nothing more than empty promises. No matter. It was what was at the very top of the tree that had caught her eye.

A big shiny star that looked absolutely magical and just like the one she'd seen at her elementary school when she'd been five.

That Christmas she remembered well.

That Christmas she'd gotten caught up in the excitement of her classmates, in the whole spirit of Christmas. Prior to then she hadn't even been sure if she'd known what Christmas or Santa had even been about. She'd written a rudimentary letter to Santa and even crawled up in his lap when he'd come to her classroom. Packed back in her things she had a Polaroid photo of that moment that she'd kept hidden away over the years for some crazy reason. Probably a reminder of what lay ahead when one got one's hopes up and believed in things that weren't real.

With excitement she'd told Santa of what she'd wanted more than anything and he'd told her to be a good girl and come Christmas morning she'd find her surprise under the tree.

She'd been as good as gold. Better than any five-year-old had ever been, surely. She'd gone to bed on Christmas Eve full of hope and had barely been able to sleep because she'd been sure she'd wake up to a pile of goodies but mainly to the pair of new sneakers she'd desperately wanted. Her others had been hand-me-downs and had grown too small. A new pair of stylish pink hightops for school was going to be a breeze with how good she'd been.

Only there had been no surprise. Or even a tree. Her mother had claimed the entire holiday was nothing more than a scam and she wasn't spending hard-earned money on something as ridiculous as putting a tree inside their tiny apartment.

When her mother had found her crying, she'd complained that Christmas was a rich man's holiday invented to make poor parents like her look bad and that

Trinity should feel ashamed for making her feel bad. Then she'd gone off and drunk until she'd passed out.

The same as she did the other three hundred and sixty-four days of the year. Only without Trinity having set herself up with false hopes that the day might bring something different.

She had stopped believing. Right then and there at five years old she'd quit believing in Christmas and Santa. Sure, she'd still gone through the motions at school and, after she'd graduated from college, at work. But she'd never believed the holiday to be anything more than commercialized hype meant to build false hopes and to disappoint. How absolutely fitting had it been that Chase had broken her heart at a Christmas party?

"Stars are magic," Riley said from beside her, pulling her back from the past to the present, obviously clueless about where her thoughts had gone. How could he know? Although she'd revealed more to him than to any other person ever, she'd rather die than have anyone know the true depth of her shame.

"Just like the star that led the wise men and the ones that guide sailors through the sea," he continued, his voice low, mesmerizing. "They lead us where we need to go if only we'll follow. Anywhere in particular you'd like to go, princess?"

Trying to keep her cynicism to a minimum and any dream of going somewhere magical well tamped down, Trinity looked at him. "It's just a cheap piece of glass and tiny light bulbs."

"Use your imagination."

"I don't have one."

"Sure you do." He laced their fingers. "Close your

eyes and picture that star, Trinity. Picture it leading you where you want to go."

"That's the most ridiculous thing I've ever heard." So why were her eyelids so darned heavy all of a sudden?

"Do it," he ordered in his Dr. Williams voice.

"You're crazy."

"About you."

That was twice he'd implied he had feelings for her. Trinity glared. "You're not going to run off when I close my eyes, are you?"

"You couldn't run me off. I'm right where I want to be."

"At the mall, shopping?" She gave him a doubtful once-over. "You sure you're straight?"

"With you," he clarified, shaking his head at her. "And if you'd like me to give a demonstration of my straightness, I'll gladly do so."

She gulped back the image of Riley proving to her that he preferred the opposite sex. Even when she was tired and irritated at him, the man could send her libido through the roof. Wow.

"Fine." She closed her eyes and did as he said. Or tried to. The image of his straightness refused to budge from her mind.

"Do you see where you want to go?"

"Oh, yeah, I see where I want to go and you offered to take me there, but for some reason I'm still quite hungry and there's no food in sight."

He laughed then surprised her by leaning forward to drop a kiss on her lips. Just a quick peck, but a kiss all the same. Had he read her thoughts?

"Come on, Scrooge," he relented, not sounding angry

but definitely not his usual happy-go-lucky self. "I'll feed you."

Guilt hit her. He was trying to be nice. It wasn't his fault she was being so otherwise.

"Hey." She feigned surprise, wanting his sparkle back. "I take back everything. That star thing worked!"

After staring at her a brief second, he grinned. "I never thought it wouldn't. Glad to know you were imagining me kissing you."

Wondering if he'd just played her with his probably feigned disappointment, she shook her head. "Keep telling yourself that, lover boy, but it's the promise that you're finally going to feed me that I referred to."

His grin way too endearing, he lifted her hand to his lips and kissed her fingertips. "You keep telling yourself that you weren't imagining my arms as where you want to be but I'm going to prove otherwise to you."

Unfortunately, Trinity couldn't argue with him because she feared he was right.

Trinity managed to make it through the next week without Riley dragging her shopping again. Thank goodness.

However, that didn't keep him from dragging her to the local soup kitchen where everyone greeted him by name. They helped serve over a hundred meals and whether it was in the name of the Christmas spirit or whatever, Trinity felt good about doing so and promised herself that she'd sign on to help on a regular basis. Not only that, she'd look for other charitable places where she could volunteer.

Of course, with Christmas being only a week away she couldn't escape the festivities. Who would have guessed that people who lived at the beach would be so into the ho, ho, ho swing of things?

At work, everyone was wearing Christmas print scrub tops and a few of the docs had Christmas ties, Riley included.

Having just returned to the nurses' station and spotting him, she rolled her eyes at the tie currently around his neck. "Seriously? You have a reindeer with a light-up nose on your tie? That's what you wore while you saw patients at your office all day?"

Waggling his brows, he grinned. "Yep, I'm quite disappointed that no one asked me to guide their sleigh tonight." He shifted to where he could look behind her at her bottom. "How about you, princess? You want me to light up your world and guide your sleigh tonight?"

That he could light up her world she had no doubt. In the past week she'd smiled and laughed more than she had...well, maybe ever. The man was a nut. And brilliant. And kind. And generous. And...

She was getting way too dependent on him. It was barely a week since he'd kissed her under the mistletoe at the hospital Christmas party and every free waking hour had been spent with him. When she wasn't with him, she was thinking of him, dreaming of him.

"Sorry, I'm fresh out of sleighs and there's not a bit of fog in sight."

If spending a week with him could have her feeling so clingy, she really needed to get a hold of herself before she did something silly. Like fall in love with him. That would be nothing short of a tragedy.

And something she needed to guard against.

"This Santa is flexible. How about we grab a bite to eat then catch that new Christmas movie?"

"Not tonight."

His smile morphed into a frown. "You have other plans?"

Trying to keep a straight face because he read her way too easily, she nodded.

"Am I invited?"

Was he invited? What kind of response was that to a woman saying she had other plans? Really, the man was too much.

"Do you want to be invited?"

"If you're going to be there? Yes, I want an invitation. A VIP pass even."

Although she was pretty sure she'd just scolded herself for being so dependent on him, she found she couldn't say no, didn't really want to because to say no would mean depriving herself of the twinkle in his eye, the mischief in his grin, the wit in his words.

"Fine. You can go with me."

He grinned and she wondered if that meant he'd known he'd get his way all along. "Where are we going, princess?"

She had no clue because she'd just made up that she had other plans in a panicky moment. She should have known better.

"It's a surprise." To her too since she probably would have just gone to her place for grilled cheese sandwiches and a rerun of some TV series. She still might.

"Aw, are you taking me caroling?" he teased.

She squinted at him in a forced glare. "That would be a surprise, now, wouldn't it? But, no, I'm not a caroler. That would contradict that whole don't-like-Christmas thing I have going."

"But you do sing," he pointed out, leaning against the counter.

"In my shower doesn't count."

"I'd like to be the judge of that for myself. You could give me a private viewing tonight. Now, that would be a surprise."

She rolled her eyes again and ignored him and the images of them in the shower flashing through her mind.

"You also sing karaoke," he reminded her.

"Only under the influence of alcohol, which I'd never knowingly do." She made a pretense of being busy.

"It's okay to let loose every once in a while and just enjoy yourself."

"I don't need alcohol to enjoy myself." She winced at how harsh her voice had been. She hadn't meant to bite his head off, yet she definitely had. Unable to just stand still, she headed to a patient room. Anything to escape him.

Unfortunately he followed her, catching her just outside the door. "I didn't say you did. I was just saying it was okay for you to relax and enjoy life. Talk to me."

She didn't want to talk. They were at work. Only Karen was near, but anyone could see them, could hear them if they wanted to eavesdrop. Even if they'd been in private she wouldn't have wanted to have this discussion, but she sure didn't here. She closed her eyes, took a deep breath. "Sorry."

"Okay." He sounded confused. "You want to explain why you jumped down my throat on that one?"

She shook her head. No, she didn't want to go there. Not at any point in the next century or so.

He appeared to weigh his options. "Okay, I'll let it slide."

They both heard his unspoken "for now".

Trinity pulled the covers off Jewel Hendrix's legs to asses them for edema.

"They're only swollen a little compared to what they were when I checked into this joint," the seventy-two-year-old woman with end-stage congestive heart failure said a bit breathily. "I can actually move my toes again."

She wiggled them back and forth.

On arrival in the emergency department, she'd been retaining so much fluid that her skin had been too tight for her to flex her toes. She'd had weeping from her skin on her shins and calves and had had crackles in her lungs. Had she not been brought to the hospital, she would have drowned in her own body fluids.

"There's still enough fluid that I can't make out your pedal pulses, though." Hopefully after another round of diuretics the swelling would go down even more.

The woman glanced at her feet. "Honey, this is a good ankle day in my book." She paused to catch her breath. "I'm pretty sure if y'all would let me up out of this bed, I could even get these boogers into a pair of shoes. Most days I feel like one of Cinderella's ugly stepsisters trying to shove my monstrosity into a glass slipper."

Trinity smiled at her patient. She really liked Jewel. The older woman had spunk.

"What about you? Some lucky fellow slip a glass slipper onto your foot and make you feel just like a princess?"

Why was it that the elderly felt they had a right to

ask questions about one's private life? Why was it that Trinity felt obligated to answer the feisty older woman?

Hoping her face was unreadable, she raised her foot up from the floor to display her solid white nursing shoes. "No glass slipper for me."

"A pity."

"Not really." Trinity slipped the skin protectors back around Jewel's feet to prevent skin breakdown and positioned her feet on the pillows to keep them elevated. "I don't need a man to slip my foot into a glass slipper. I'm way too practical for that. Besides, with my luck a glass slipper would only shatter and cut my foot up anyway."

Trinity smiled at the woman, but Jewel's face was pinched into a frown.

"Maybe the wrong quality of men have been attempting to slip glass slippers onto your feet. You need to upgrade."

Ha. No man had been attempting to slip a glass slipper onto her foot, but she wouldn't admit that to Jewel. Besides, she had no right to complain. Riley treated her as if she really were the princess he often called her. She had to admit that most of the time she liked the attention he showered on her. Who needed glass slippers and a Prince Charming when you had a handsome cardiologist trying to woo you into Christmas cheer?

Trinity tucked the bed sheet and white blanket around her patient's elevated legs. "I'll keep that in mind the next time a Prince Charming asks to see my feet."

The woman chuckled. "I like you."

Trinity shot the woman another smile. "You can sweet-talk me all you want, but I'm still going to give you your medication."

"I never thought you wouldn't." The woman practically cackled. "When's that handsome doctor of mine going to be here?"

"Dr. Williams should be by any time. He was here earlier, but got called to the cardiac lab for a procedure." She'd only caught a glimpse of him, but a glimpse had been all it had taken to get her heart racing. Especially with how he'd winked at her when their eyes had met. Karen had teased her on that one, but Trinity hadn't really cared. Most of the time he made her feel good. And confused.

Although everyone at the hospital had accepted that they were a couple, Trinity just wasn't sure exactly what they were. Other than a few brief kisses and holding her hand, he barely touched her. What was his game? "I expect he'll be finishing up some time soon."

Did she mean with the patient or with her?

Jewel sighed. "I'd like to be home for Christmas. Maybe he'll let me leave this evening."

"Maybe," Trinity said, adjusting the setting on Jewel's intravenous pump. The woman wasn't receiving any fluids currently as her problem was fluid overload. However, her diuretics were being given intravenously and Trinity had just hung a new bag of the medication. "But I doubt it. You were a really sick lady when you got here yesterday morning. We really need to get more fluid off before you can go home."

Jewel eyed the bag of medication. "But I'm a lot better than I was and that stuff there is going to help even more."

"True, but you're also heavily medicated and Dr. Williams will want to keep a close check on your electrolytes for at least another day, probably longer. Your medication can deplete your potassium and if that happens, a whole new set of problems could occur."

"We can't have that."

"Which is why I don't think he'll discharge you any time soon. Or at least not until after you've had your echocardiogram."

Jewel sighed. "That's the ultrasound thing with the sticky stuff on my chest?"

"Yes, ma'am. No pain involved." Trinity entered the data from her assessment of Jewel into the in-room computer and that she'd begun administration of the medication ordered.

"How's my most beautiful patient doing this evening?"

The old woman's brow rose. "I'm your only patient? A brilliant doctor like you? That's surprising and a bit worrisome."

Riley laughed and winked at the older woman. "You're a quick one, Jewel."

"That I am." The woman beamed.

Trinity smothered a smile and clicked to save and sign the data she'd entered.

"You going to let me go home today?"

Riley shook his head. "Now, why would I do that when your nurse just told you the reasons why you should stay?"

Jewel shrugged her heavy shoulders. "I was just checking."

"Anyone ever tell you what a testy thing you are?" Riley teased the older woman, pulling his stethoscope from his pocket and cleaning the diaphragm with an alcohol swab.

"Only my husband." The woman's face took on a happy glow. "God bless him."

Riley laughed and placed his stethoscope on Jewel's chest.

The breathy woman watched his every move. Glancing up, she noticed that Trinity also watched his every move.

Jewel motioned towards Riley then waggled her drawn-on eyebrows.

Noticing the movement, Riley glanced up, caught just enough that he glanced back and forth between them. "Okay, you two, what are you cooking up?"

Trinity shook her head. No way was she going there. Jewel would have to do her matchmaking elsewhere because as sweet as Riley was to her and as fine as he seemed to be with everyone thinking they were a couple, she didn't fool herself that he was a Prince Charming who was going to slip a pair of glass slippers onto her feet.

Or even a pair of pink hightop sneakers.

She'd do well to remember that.

CHAPTER EIGHT

LETTING HIS GAZE soak up the sight of Trinity in her dark navy scrubs, Riley stepped up beside where she worked at the nurses' station. "Dr. Stanley is having a small impromptu get-together tomorrow night, just dinner and drinks, to celebrate the holidays."

Trinity looked briefly at Riley then went back to studying the computer monitor.

"Would you like to go?"

"No, thank you," she immediately replied, without another glance his way.

Tempted to scream with frustration, Riley sighed. "Do you know any words other than those?"

"Yes."

"Great." He rubbed his hands together in glee. "You really do. We should get you in the habit of using them more often. Let's practice. Trinity, will you go to a Christmas dinner party with me tomorrow night?"

She arched a brow at him. "You want me to be a yes-girl?"

Did he?

"I want you to be an open-minded girl who answers questions based on more than her preconceived notion that she doesn't like Christmas and wants no part of any celebration of it."

"You're missing the point completely."

He leaned against the desktop and stared down at her. "Which is?"

"That I really don't like Christmas so why would I purposely choose to celebrate it?"

Had a more stubborn woman ever walked the face of the earth?

"Okay, fine." He sighed. "We won't go to my boss's Christmas party that he invited me to and mentioned bringing you with me." Was it wrong that he was laying on the guilt as thick as could be? "What would you prefer to do tomorrow night?"

"Just because I don't want to go, it doesn't mean you can't go, Riley. You go ahead and have enough fun for both of us."

Ouch. "You want me to go to a party without you?"

"If it's a Christmas party? Yes." She put a lot of emphasis on the word. "I do."

What woman wanted her man to go to a party without her? Or maybe she didn't think of him as her man? He'd purposely fought to keep the physical side of their relationship at bay because she was so obstinate she'd be likely to use them having sex against him. If he went to a party without her, she'd likely do the same.

He shook his head. "What if I'd rather be with you?"

"Then maybe we could go for a walk on the beach," she surprised him by suggesting. He'd expected her to insist on him going, on her insisting she had other plans. She rarely said yes without him having to sweet-talk her. He didn't like it and kept waiting for her to quit playing such games. Maybe she finally had.

"To be so close to the Gulf," she continued. "I've barely been there."

"My place okay?"

Without looking at him, she nodded. "Yes." She put great emphasis on the word. "That would be fine."

Wow. Maybe they really had reached a turning point. Good, because keeping his hands to himself was growing more and more difficult. He wanted her.

"You want me to grill some salmon fillets? We could walk on the beach afterwards then sit on my deck and enjoy a glass of wine?"

Make love under the stars, in his bed, his shower especially, because ever since he'd mentioned her giving him a private viewing he hadn't been able to get the image from his mind. Or maybe they'd just sit on his deck and talk. Just so long as she let her guard down long enough for them to enjoy the night, he'd be a happy camper, sex or not.

"I don't drink," she said, but at least she hadn't said no.

"Cool. We'll sip juice on my deck." Other than the occasional glass of wine, he generally didn't drink either, so wine or juice wasn't a big deal to him. Plus, he wanted a completely clear mind if and when they touched. "I'll pick up some fillets on my way home and let them marinate tonight. You want a spinach salad? Maybe some sautéed asparagus in butter sauce?"

Trinity blinked up at him. "Are you for real? I just made you grilled cheese for your surprise dinner the other night."

"Pinch me and see." He waggled his brows, feeling lighter than he had in days. He hadn't realized just how frustrated he'd grown. "I'll pick the spot."

Her lips twitched with a smile she couldn't hold back and his entire insides warmed. Finally they were making real progress.

"I should do just that. Only I'd have to pick the spot."

"I'm game. Anywhere in particular you'd prefer to start? I could offer a few suggestions. Maybe give you a few pointers on my preferences?"

She looked up as if she was going to roll her eyes, but her smile was now full blown. "You really are crazy, you know?"

He thought about reminding her of exactly what he was crazy about, but just grinned, happier than he should be that she'd agreed without him having to talk her into doing so.

"I don't want to keep you from your boss's party, Riley," she relented, but he could tell she wasn't enthused at the prospect. "Not if it's something you want to go to."

"Not a problem." His insides felt light. "I like our plans better anyway."

Her smile made her eyes sparkle with the brilliance of twinkling green Christmas lights. "You're sure?"

"Positive."

"I feel guilty that you're going to cook for me. Is there something I can do?"

He nodded.

She arched a brow.

"Come with hunger in your belly and a smile in your heart."

She hesitated a moment then met his gaze head on, making his heart stutter a time or two.

"That's all you want me to bring?"

A dozen different responses ran through his mind.

An open mind. A spirit full of Christmas. Open arms to embrace him. A willing heart. He settled for something simple.

"For now."

Okay, the man was really too good to be true. Because Riley had not only cooked for her, he'd lit candles.

Candles.

At no point in her life had a man given her a candle-lit dinner. Actually, never had a man cooked for her either.

Riley had done both and was merrily singing while he did so.

What was this? A romantic seduction? Didn't he know he could have had her at any point over the past week?

She'd like to think not, but truly, had Riley pushed, she'd have invited him into her bed any of the nights that he'd seen her into her apartment then left with little more than a kiss.

Not only were there candles on the dining table, but they were scattered around the room as well. Plus, his tree sparkled with the thousands of lights they'd strung around the branches. Garlands hung over the doorways. Gorgeous burgundy and gold ribbon bows accented the centers and twined outwards. A nativity scene was spread out over a coffee table. His sofa cushions had been replaced with ones with a smiling Santa on them.

He even wore a "Kiss Santa" apron tied around his waist.

Leaning against the deck railing, she shook her head. "I do have to wonder how old you are sometimes."

A breeze ruffling his hair, he glanced up from where

he stood at the grill. "A person is only as old as they feel so I'm about…thirteen."

Smiling, she glanced through the glass windows making up the back of his house and door leading into his open living and dining area again. Her eyes caught on the toy train set on the floor beneath the Christmas tree. Her lips twitched. "Gee, I was thinking more along the lines of six. Maybe seven."

"Nah." He shook his head, moved away from the grill long enough to plop a kiss on her lips. "Six- and seven-year-old boys couldn't care less about girls and I definitely am into girls. Specifically, I'm into you."

Trinity's belly did a few somersaults. "Point taken, and I'm glad."

Because as scared as she was of getting hurt, she was honest enough to admit that she wouldn't have wanted to miss out on being the center of his attention. For however long it lasted, Riley was into her and that was a glorious thing. Her defenses might warn she should run while she still could but another part of her admitted that it was already too late.

Perhaps it had been too late from the moment at the Christmas party when she'd looked into those devilish blue eyes and he'd assured her he was a man who aimed to please. No one had ever made her feel the way he did. Worthwhile. Wanted.

"You look beautiful, by the way."

Point in case. Trinity's cheeks burned. He was always complimenting her, making her look in the mirror and wonder what he saw that she didn't. That no one other than him had ever seen. Because despite their nine-month relationship, Chase had never called her beautiful. Neither had he ever made her feel as if she was.

110 AFTER THE CHRISTMAS PARTY...

Why had she fancied herself in love with him?

Because she hadn't known any better? Hadn't known what a good man was really like and she'd been settling for what had been right in front of her rather than looking for something more? Something real?

Something like Riley.

No, she wasn't in love with him, although it would be so easy to fall in love with him. The man was a phenom. She didn't know how any woman could spend any amount of time with him and not fancy herself in love with him. He was that kind, that considerate, that witty, that sexy, that everything.

"I hope you're hungry, princess." He lifted a tin-foil-wrapped salmon fillet off the grill.

"Starved."

Starved for food, but maybe for much more than she'd bargained for. Nothing in her life had prepared her for Riley. She was supposed to be taking charge of her life, learning to deal with her Christmas aversion. She was not supposed to be becoming so entangled with a man she'd have a difficult time ever letting go of, and yet she didn't regret being here with him. She cherished every precious second of his company, of his attention.

She'd given up pretending otherwise.

"Starved?" He grinned. "That's my girl."

His girl. He didn't care who knew, who saw them together, or who saw him brushing his knuckles across her cheek or just giving her hand a quick squeeze. If anything, he acted possessive, as if he wanted everyone who saw them to know they were together. As if he was proud she was with him.

It had been months before Chase had wanted anyone

at the hospital to be aware that they were dating and then he'd acted more embarrassed than proud.

"Why are you so nice to me?" she mused out loud.

"Huh?" Obviously, he had no clue what she meant. Which made her happy inside. He wasn't putting on airs or trying to impress her, just being himself.

"I'm just curious why you're so nice to me."

"I already told you the answer to that, princess. More than once."

"What's that?"

"I like you." He smiled and she deep-down knew he believed what he said. He liked her. "A lot."

"This is good," Trinity praised twenty minutes later, the lemony grilled salmon practically melting in her mouth. "Much better than my grilled cheese the other night. I think you missed your calling."

"I happened to like your grilled cheese the other night, although perhaps not the butt-kicking at chess that followed." He grinned. "You really think I should give up cardiology and cook for a living?"

She snorted. "When you word it that way, probably not, but you are a very talented man and I am well aware that I barely won that chess game."

"Glad you noticed and appreciate my efforts."

"Oh, I notice." Every detail about him. She took another bite. "You have a beautiful place, Riley."

"I like it. When I was looking to buy, I knew I'd make an offer on this one the moment I stepped inside, even though it's a little further from the hospital than I'd intended. It felt like I was coming home."

She glanced out the windows towards the sea. "Great view."

"It's better tonight than usual."

But when she turned to him, he wasn't looking at the gulf. He was looking at her.

Heat infused her entire body. "You don't have to say things like that, you know."

"I know. I want to."

"Why?"

"Why?" He sounded confused. "Why wouldn't I?"

"I don't know. You're just always complimenting me and I don't want you to feel it's necessary."

"But complimenting you is necessary. Very necessary."

She wanted to ask why again, but didn't want to sound like a broken record. So she smiled. With Riley, when in doubt about what to do, smiling seemed to work best. "This house suits you. Functional, beautiful—"

"Christmasy?" he interjected, grinning.

"Christmasy," she agreed, unable to deny his claim. He was everything Christmas should be. Everything that Christmas had never been. Not for her. But everything he did made a long-suppressed part of her memory pull forward.

Enough so that she experienced a twinge of panic, but the evening was too nice to let doubt ruin it.

They finished eating and together cleared away the dishes, stacking them in the sink. Trinity tried to load them into the dishwasher, but he shook his head.

"Not now. Let's go for that walk on the beach. I've been looking forward to it since you first mentioned doing so earlier."

"Okay." She set her plate down on the marble countertop and picked up the jacket he'd set out earlier for their walk as the wind was brisk. "You talked me into it."

Putting on his own lightweight jacket, he laughed. "That's my girl."

As much as she kept telling herself that she wasn't in love with this man, that she wouldn't fall in love with him, she couldn't argue with his statement.

She was his girl.

Indisputably.

Hand in hand, Riley and Trinity walked along the beach. Ignoring how much he wanted Trinity was getting more and more difficult. He didn't want to rush her, didn't want to make wild assumptions, but from the moment she'd arrived all he'd wanted to do was pull her into his arms.

Her mind stimulated him.

Her quick wit stimulated him.

Her curvy little body stimulated him.

It was the latter that was currently tearing his resolve into bits. He felt as if he was in a constant state of stimulation.

He couldn't recall ever feeling this way. Not even when he'd been a randy teenager.

Letting go of his hand, she'd ran ahead of him, laughing as the waves lapped at her bare feet. She turned to beckon him to join her. Wind whipped at her hair.

Temptation whipped at his soul.

What he wanted was to push her down in the surf, rip her clothes off and make love to her right then and there, with the waves crashing around their naked bodies.

He swallowed, watched her dance around in the white foam.

"Riley, hurry," she called. The water crashed around

her ankles and she laughed, looking and sounding freer than he recalled ever seeing her.

Like a child set loose to play.

Like the most tantalizing woman to ever tempt man.

"I ate too much to hurry," he called, enjoying watching her play too much to rush.

"Right." She laughed then plopped down just beyond the water's reach, her toes stretched out towards the sea, tempting the water to move closer and closer.

"You know you're going to get wet, right? Then you'll be cold."

She shrugged. "At the moment I don't care. This is wonderful."

He glanced out to sea then back at the smiling woman leaning back as if offering herself to the moon shining above them.

If so, he was jealous of the moon.

Because he wanted her to offer herself to him that way.

Every way.

He wanted her to come to him, for her to initiate their lovemaking, for her to have no regrets and for him to have no worries that he'd talked her into something she hadn't really wanted.

He'd thought himself a patient man, but looking at her body stretched out under the bright moonlight, the surf nipping at her toes, he had none.

"Besides, if I get cold, you'll warm me up, right?"

He hadn't realized she was watching him. He gulped back the knot her words caused to form in his throat and willed the one forming in his pants to go away.

"Riley?"

"Hmm?"

"Are you afraid to join me?"

Terrified. Because getting close to her might mean losing control and seducing her right out of her panties. What would his neighbors think? Although, honestly, he wasn't sure how many were even home at this time of year. A lot of the houses along this stretch were owned by wealthy snowbirds looking for an escape.

"Scared you'll get wet?" she teased, digging her fingers into the sand beside her.

"Nope." To prove his point, he sat down next to her on the sand. "But I should warn you that I'm very turned on and perhaps you should get up and run while you can because what I really want to do would get me arrested."

Arrested? Trinity blinked, wondering if she'd misheard him over the waves. "Do what?"

"You heard me. Just what I said. You're beautiful and totally do it for me. I look at you and I want you. I have wanted you from the first moment I set eyes on you propped up against that hotel ballroom wall. Tonight, here on the beach, I want you so badly I may explode from it. I feel weak. If I did with you what I want to do with you, I'd be arrested."

He wanted her. Really wanted her. A heady sensation, but the other thing he'd said played in her mind.

"I make you weak?" She didn't want to make him or any man weak. Especially not when he made her feel strong, stronger than she recalled ever feeling.

He picked up her hand, pressed it to where his heart beat. "Does that feel as if you make me weak?"

His heart pounded beneath her fingertips. She shook her head.

"My resolve is what's weak. You make me feel alive,"

he clarified. "As if everything I do is bigger, brighter, more than anything I've ever done."

That she understood because it's how he made her feel. It amazed her that he could possibly feel the same. How could he when that seemed so unlikely? "I do?"

He nodded.

"I want you, Trinity, but I didn't mean to tell you like this."

She glanced around at the beach. Although there were other houses along the stretch of beach, they were essentially alone. The moon shone bright above them. The sea crashed foamy white waves that played a perfect love song. He'd just cooked her a delicious dinner and he'd lit candles. She couldn't imagine anything more romantic, more seductive.

"What's wrong with this? With this very moment?"

"Earlier I thought..." he shook his head. "It's too soon."

He was probably right. Less than two weeks was too soon. Still, they'd been together every night and if you put that on regular dating terms of weekend dates, they'd been seeing each other for months. Or was she just reaching?

Probably.

Because her hand had moved from his chest to his face. The grit of sand still lingered on her fingers but his skin was smooth, perfect.

"It's not too soon," she whispered, knowing it was true, especially when she heard his intake of breath above the crash of the waves. "But I should warn you that if we did, you'd be disappointed."

"Never."

She laughed ironically at his faith. If only. "I wish that was true, but I'm not very good at…well, you know."

"Sex?"

Staring at where her hand caressed his jaw, she nodded. "I can pretty much guarantee that you won't want me any more once we do."

This time it was he who laughed. "You'd be wrong."

"Again, I wish that was true."

"Why?"

Could she write him a thesis on all the reasons why? Things like that he made her feel good about herself? That he made her believe in things that she shouldn't believe in? That he'd taken away the loneliness that had iced her insides for so long that she'd believed the coldness was a permanent part of who she was?

"Because I like you," she said instead, using his usual response to sum up all the emotions bubbling inside her. "A lot."

In the moonlight, she saw his mouth curve upwards.

"Good to know," he admitted, taking her hand. "I was beginning to wonder if this relationship was one-sided."

"Is that what we're doing? Having a relationship?" Not that it didn't feel like a relationship. It did. Plus he carried on at the hospital as if they were. But, still, there was no one around but the two of them and she wanted a straight answer from him.

"If you have to ask me that, I'm doing something very wrong," he teased, scratching his head as if trying to figure out what that something might be.

"I…I just wasn't sure." Which sounded quite lame at the moment, with how his eyes searched hers. Even in the moonlight she could see desire flickering in the blue depths.

"After the past two weeks you aren't sure that I'm totally fascinated by you and want to spend every second of my time with you?"

Wow. That's all that her brain could register. Just wow. Wow. Wow. Riley's words seemed so foreign, so far-fetched, yet she heard his sincerity, saw the truth in the way he looked at her. He looked at her as she'd never been looked at, as if she was the most precious being on earth.

"I'm scared," she heard herself say, knowing her words were as true as his, shocked, though, that she was admitting her fear to him. Wasn't that exposing just how vulnerable she really was?

"Don't be scared of me, Trinity. I'd never intentionally hurt you."

Intentionally. Which meant she likely would be hurt at some point down the line. Her life had taught her to expect no less. But she wasn't going to hold back, wasn't going to let the past or fear dictate who she was. Not when it came to Riley. Was she?

At this moment she was a woman sitting on a romantic beach, touching a fantasy man who was quickly encompassing her whole world.

He wanted to be here, with her. He thought she was beautiful, he wanted her, and he didn't mind telling her, showing her.

When he was with her she didn't get the impression that he wanted to be anywhere except right with her. When he looked at her she didn't get the impression that he wished she were someone else.

He wanted *her*.

He lifted her hand to his lips, kissed her fingertips.

"I have sand on my fingers." And tears in her eyes. Why was she crying?

"Doesn't matter." He kissed the top of her hand, gently turned her arm to press his lips to her wrist, then he kissed her there. Gentle kisses where his lips lightly brushed across the tender skin, heating her blood. Brilliant kisses that made her mind go in thousands of directions, all of which involved him.

She shivered and scooted closer to him, grazed her knuckles across his clean-shaven jaw. "Smooth."

He chuckled. "The better to kiss you without worrying about scratching you."

"I'm not a dainty flower that easily wilts."

"You want scratched?"

"I want kissed."

"I'm a man who aims to please."

When his lips covered hers, he didn't kiss her with the gentle pressure he'd kissed her goodnight with each night. No, he kissed her with the mouth of a man who was hungry. Hungry and wanting to devour her.

As if he wanted her so much he couldn't not kiss her that way.

The sensation was heady.

Trinity's head spun she felt so light, so good, so unreal.

Riley was unreal.

Because no way was such a beautiful man kissing her as if he couldn't get enough, as if he wanted, no, needed, everything she could give him.

She wanted to give him everything.

But if she did, would it be the beginning of the end, the way it had been with Chase?

Would Riley find her so lacking between the sheets that he wouldn't want her any more and would wonder why he'd ever thought he had thought her something special?

Or did sex even matter that much to him?

His mouth moved lower, to her neck, trailing hot kisses, making love to her skin.

Um, yeah, this was a man who cared about sex. No doubt about it.

Which meant she was in big trouble.

CHAPTER NINE

RILEY FELT THE difference in Trinity's response and pulled back. "You okay? Am I coming on too strong? I didn't mean to move too fast."

He'd known better than to rush things, but he'd thought... No matter what he'd thought. The reality was they'd only known each other for two weeks and he had moved too fast. She was scooting away from him, standing, brushing the sand off her clothes, and was a million miles away from him.

"You're fine."

Fine? Not the adjective he wanted to be called when he was on fire for her and had just been kissing her with a great amount of gusto.

Mindless kisses that had been all about feeling and emotion and had had little to do with thought or intentions.

"The wind just felt a little chilly. That's all. I want to finish our walk now."

Just what every man wanted to hear when he was on the verge of making love to a woman he was crazy about. When he'd been overcome with passion and she'd...she'd decided she wanted to finish their walk. Oh, yeah, he'd pushed too soon. Only had he really?

She'd wanted him, too. Had he done something wrong? Or was she playing games with him?

"Okay, we'll walk." He stood, brushed his clothes off, and took her hand.

He wasn't sure she wanted him holding her hand either, but he wasn't going to let her shut him out after the kiss they'd just shared.

She'd told him she was scared. Was that why she'd pulled away?

She'd also told him that she wasn't very good at sex.

Based on how she kissed him, he'd say she couldn't be more wrong.

But maybe she really believed otherwise. He was reaching, but there had to be some reason why she was now lost in thought instead of in his arms, and he sure didn't want to believe it was that she was a tease. The vulnerability he sensed within her assured him that wasn't the case.

"You're a very good kisser."

Her head jerked toward him.

"An amazing kisser," he added, seeing the doubt in her eyes. Hell, someone had really done a number on her.

"You're the one who's a great kisser." She shrugged as if it was no big deal, but he could see that his praise pleased her. "I just follow your lead."

"Thanks for saying so, but you don't give yourself enough credit. You drive me wild, Trinity."

She gave him a weak smile and squeezed his hand. "Thank you."

"You're welcome." As much as his body urged him to pick up where they'd left off, to take her in his arms and kiss her until she was breathless and begging for the release he craved, he just clasped her hand in his and walked.

Patience might not be his virtue, but some things were worth the wait. He had no doubt that when he and Trinity made love, and they *would* make love, the wait would be worth having the patience of Job.

How could her schedule have been changed? No one ever wanted to work on Christmas, so surely she wouldn't have been randomly taken off the schedule?

She stared at the holiday work schedule. Her name was not on the twenty-fifth anywhere. Christmas Eve, yes, but not the big awful day itself.

She had been on that list. How had her name been taken off?

"What are you looking at?" Karen asked, stepping up behind Trinity and looking over her shoulder to see what had her so captivated.

"There was a message in my inbox about last-minute holiday schedule changes and for everyone to recheck the hours they'd be working."

"Yeah, I saw that."

"I'm no longer scheduled for Christmas Day."

"Lucky girl."

"Not lucky girl." Because if she wasn't working, she had to go with Riley to his family dinner. Not that there wasn't a teeny tiny part of her that wanted to go, to meet the people he spoke of with such love, but the thought of a Christmas Day dinner was too much. Plus she'd have to buy them presents. Not that she was such a tightwad that she minded spending the money, but what the heck would she buy people she'd never met and who were from such a different social background from her own?

"You sound as if having Christmas Day off is a bad thing." Karen grinned at her. "Enjoy yourself, spend some time with family."

Time with family? Ha. Her only family had been her mother and she'd died several years ago from liver problems.

But Riley's family?

"Or that good-looking man you're dating. Now, there's a way to spend Christmas Day. Unwrapping really great packages." Karen waggled her brows.

Panic tightened Trinity's throat. She glanced at the schedule again. "You're supposed to work. Let me take your place."

Karen looked at her as if she was crazy. "Why would you do that?"

"Because I moved here from out of state, remember? I don't have any family. I'll be by myself if I'm not working. I should work and you go enjoy your day with your family."

Karen shook her head. "No way. Pay for Christmas Day is always double time and I need the extra money. I'd put in to work and was glad for the schedule change as I'm helping put my kid sister through school. Besides, I seriously doubt Dr. Williams is going to let you spend Christmas Day alone."

Okay, so convincing Karen to swap with her wasn't going to work. Maybe one of the other cardiac nurses would swap with her.

No such luck.

Trinity couldn't work out why not a single one of the nurses scheduled to work on Christmas Day preferred to have the holiday itself off. Not a single one of them was willing to let her work instead of them. Unbelievable.

What was up with this hospital anyway? Didn't they have any Christmas spirit? They were supposed to want to be at home, to be with their families, to…not be like her.

Annoyed at herself, she went into a patient room and forced a smile onto her face for Jewel's benefit.

"Not working."

"Huh?" she asked, confused by her patient's immediate comment. "What's not working?"

"That fake smile." Jewel pursed her lips. "I take it you still haven't found that pair of glass slippers?"

"If you recall our conversation, you'll remember that I don't want glass slippers. Way too impractical for a practical girl like me."

Jewel snorted. "You can talk big all you want, but when I look at you I see the truth."

Scary thought, but somehow she believed Jewel really did see more when she looked than most people did. As if age had given her insight beyond the surface.

"What truth would that be?"

"That you're a romantic through and through."

Trinity made a face then put her hand across Jewel's wrinkled forehead as if taking her skin temperature. "Uh-oh. I think we'd better call your doctor because you're delirious."

"And you, my dearie, aren't fooling this old gal. You crave romance."

Wondering at why she sounded as out of breath as her patient, Trinity shook her head. "Wrong. Pink hightops were my dream shoes, not glass slippers. I run from romance."

Riley paused outside Jewel's door, fascinated by the conversation he was overhearing. Perhaps he should feel guilty for eavesdropping, but he didn't. He needed an edge with Trinity, something to push him in the right direction where she was concerned, because she confused him.

And frustrated him.

Since the night on the beach she'd gone right back behind her wall, and had also erected a barrier between them. A new barrier because he wasn't convinced there had ever been a point where she hadn't had a protective wall between them.

Except perhaps for a few moments there on the beach when she'd been touching his face. When she'd looked at him, touched him, she'd been unguarded.

He'd liked what he'd seen, what he'd felt. A lot.

He wanted that woman, that unguarded Trinity, all the time.

The one he knew was buried within her who claimed to not like Christmas, to not believe in the magic of the season. He wanted to see her laugh as she had in the surf, to let herself loose with him and just embrace life.

Not for her to beg every nurse on the schedule to let her work for them on Christmas Day so she could get out of spending the day with him.

That had almost had him losing his temper. Even now the idea that she'd do that got his hackles up. Then again, perhaps he couldn't say a thing because he'd already ensured none of them would swap with her, and without bribery.

Just because Trinity claimed not to be a romantic, it didn't mean the other nurses on the cardiac floor were immune to romance. When he'd told them he'd planned a Christmas surprise for Trinity, they'd all oohed and ahhed. Yeah, the other cardiac nurses were as much suckers for romance as…as he was.

Because he wanted to give Trinity romance and lots of it. He wanted to show her what Christmas was all about.

"Why on earth would you run from romance? Especially in a pair of pink hightops?" Jewel sounded as confused by Trinity's claim as Riley himself was.

"Because romance is all about building up expectations and making promises that won't come true, not in the real world, so of course I run."

That's exactly how she described Christmas.

"Honey, like I said before—" Riley could just see Jewel's head bobbing back and forth "—you've been hanging out with the wrong Prince Charming."

Riley frowned.

She'd been hanging out with him.

Was he the wrong Prince Charming for Trinity?

For that matter, did he even want to be a Prince Charming? It wasn't a role he'd ever envisioned for himself. He worked long hours, was dedicated to his career and would never want to do to a wife and family what his father had.

He wasn't looking for happily-ever-after, but there was something about filling Trinity's world with goodness and dreams come true that made him long for the ability to wave a magic wand and give her the world, to slip that glass slipper on her foot and be her Prince Charming.

"I like the man I've been hanging with. He's a great guy."

Riley's chest puffed out a bit at her admission. Oh,

yeah. That was him she was talking about. She liked him and thought he was a great guy.

"If he's such a great guy, where's the glass slippers on your feet and the dreamy look in your eyes?"

Leave it to Jewel to point out the harsh reality.

Trinity laughed, the sound sparkly and warming something inside Riley.

He wanted to make her laugh that way.

"He tries, Jewel, he really, really tries, but I'm damaged goods."

"Damaged goods?"

"Lots of baggage. Plus, Christmas isn't my favorite time of year."

"Not a crime, but why not?"

"Long, long story, but the most recent installment would be that my boyfriend dumped me quite publicly a couple of years ago at our hospital Christmas party. I wasn't much on the holiday prior to that, but gave up completely at that point. Nothing merry about a day that only reminds you of bad memories."

"Sounds to me like I was right. You have been dating the wrong Prince Charming." Jewel made a sound that could have been her clearing her throat or could have been her faking a gag. "Let's hope this current guy you say you like has more sense."

"Let's hope."

Trinity's voice held a dreamy quality that could only be defined as real hope. She hoped he had enough sense to be her Prince Charming? Was that it? Was he not giving her enough romance? He hadn't really tried to be romantic, just himself. Although most men would say that cooking a candlelit dinner for her should have won him more than a few romance brownie points. He'd done more for her than he'd ever done for any woman. Was it not enough?

Still, she'd given him food for thought.

He'd planned to go in, check Jewel and see if sending her home for the holidays was a remote possibility.

Instead, he walked away from the room wondering what one had to do to be Trinity's Prince Charming? Her *right* Prince Charming?

And wondering why making sure he did just that was so important when he wasn't a happily-ever-after kind of guy.

Christmas Eve. Only a few more days of this nonsense and then the world would be focused on out with the old and in with the new and how many resolutions could everyone make that they didn't really intend to keep.

Trinity could barely wait.

Sure, so far she'd made it through the holiday season with a lot fewer tears than last year.

Actually, she hadn't cried much at all, and she knew why.

Riley.

Since the Christmas party they'd been together pretty much non-stop and she hadn't had time to dwell on Christmases past.

Just Christmas present.

No way would she even consider Christmas future. She had to make it through the rest of the current holiday season first.

As in, what the heck was she going to buy his family? She'd forced herself into a few shops and hadn't found one thing that said, *Buy me because Riley's family will love me.*

How the devil was she supposed to know what to purchase for people she'd never met? She'd considered buying everything from gourmet cheese and fruit to the latest bestseller. She'd even done several late night frantic internet searches on gifts for people one didn't know.

Nothing had seemed just right.

She'd yet to see Riley today as the cardiology group he was a part of had closed up shop for the next two days, but she knew he'd be by at some point to check on his hospital patients. He was the kind of doctor who would do a round on his own patients rather than have the on-call doc do so.

"Hey, before you leave today, make sure you find me," Karen said as she came around the nurses' station. "I have a little something for you."

"You do?" Trinity asked, thankful for the little something she'd picked up for her coworker while searching for Riley's family something. The small gift was stuck inside a Christmas bag with Karen's name on it inside her purse.

"Well, yeah." Karen gave her a "duh" look. "We are friends, aren't we?"

"Well, yeah." She mimicked Karen's tone, mostly to cover the odd emotion moving through her chest. Karen had gotten her a Christmas gift. And just called them friends. "But we never discussed gifts, so I didn't expect you'd get me anything."

"What? You didn't get me anything? Guess that rules out that new Corvette I've been wanting." Karen feigned a sigh. "There's always next year."

"I didn't say I didn't get you anything," Trinity pointed out, "but you're right, there's not a Corvette sitting out in the employee parking lot with a big red bow and your name on it. At least, if there is, I'm not the one who got it for you."

Karen grinned. "Maybe we should check the parking lot out to see."

They both laughed.

"So what are your Christmas Day plans?" Karen asked, but sounded as if perhaps she already knew the answer.

"Well, unless I can convince you to let me work in your place, I'll be going with Riley to his family Christmas lunch."

"Wow. I figured you'd be spending the day with him but a family get-together? Are you two that serious?"

Heat infused Trinity's face. That serious. How did she answer that when she didn't know the answer herself? "It's just a meal."

"When a man takes a woman with him to a family holiday meal, it's never just anything. It's a big deal."

"Maybe he just felt sorry for me because I'm new in town." Yet another reason why she didn't want to go. She didn't want his pity.

"Are you kidding me? I have seen the way that man looks at you. He is smitten."

Which sounded good but also a little too good to be true. She kept expecting him to snap out of whatever spell he'd fallen under. Then where would she be? Lost.

"What are you wearing?"

Trinity shrugged. She hadn't even thought about what she'd wear. What was wrong with her? She should have thought about it. Only she was so used to just wearing hospital scrubs that she didn't give much thought to anything else.

Laughing, Karen shook her head. "Okay, so you've

no clue what you're wearing. How about gifts for Riley's family?"

If her face had been hot moments before it was deathly cold now.

"I wish I knew. I've been searching for something from the moment I realized I was going to have to go to this dinner, but what do you buy for people you've never met?"

Karen paused a moment then shrugged. "Nothing big or fancy, just some token of appreciation that says thank you for including me and, no, I'm not a total loser that your son's dragged home to meet you."

"Maybe I am a total loser when it comes to Christmas, because I don't have gifts for them and don't know what to buy."

Karen looked thoughtful then waggled her brows. "Anything at home you can re-gift?"

Re-gift? As in give away something that someone had given her once upon a time? That would be assuming that she'd received gifts over the years. She rarely had.

She winced and met her friend's gaze. "What am I going to do? I'm running out of time. Tonight, after work, is the last chance I have."

Shaking her head in mock sympathy, Karen laughed. "I guess you are going to join the throng of last-minute shoppers who are hitting the stores the minute they get off work tonight and pick something from whatever is left on the sales rack."

Trinity closed her eyes.

Go shopping for Christmas gifts on Christmas Eve.

Oh, joy to the world.

CHAPTER TEN

RILEY HAD PLANNED to spend Christmas Eve with Trinity, but obviously she'd had other ideas because when he'd asked her to come over for dinner, she'd refused.

Something she hadn't done for a while so she'd caught him off guard. He'd just assumed they'd spend Christmas Eve evening together and hadn't even considered any other possibility.

He paced across his deck, staring out at the sea. The wind was up a bit and held a chill. The waves crashed noisily against the beach, the pounding sound matching his mood.

What if Trinity refused to go with him tomorrow? What if she refused to see him on Christmas Day, period?

What kind of glass-slipper-wielding Prince Charming could he be if she wouldn't even let him have a go at her feet?

Besides which, he wasn't quite sure how he was going to pull off everything he had planned. His sports utility vehicle was packed to the brim with what he'd planned to give her, but the reality was that he might have put a whole lot of effort into something he wouldn't even be able to pull off. It wasn't as if she even had a chimney for him to shoot down. Besides, breaking and entering with her asleep in her bedroom seemed a little too stalker-ish.

He closed his eyes, breathed in the salty scent of the sea.

Where was she? What was she doing?

Surely not mourning over the idiot who'd dumped her? Ever since he'd overheard her conversation he'd wanted to strangle the guy.

And to hold her tight and never let go.

At least he understood the walls she hid behind a bit better.

Raking his fingers through his hair, Riley sighed. He didn't like feeling at a loose end. They'd only started spending time together two weeks ago. A single night away from her had him antsy?

Maybe Trinity was missing him as much as he was missing her. Only one way to find out.

He slid his hand into his pants pocket to call her. His phone started ringing before he could even press a single key.

The number on the screen had him letting out another sigh, this one full of relief and something akin to pleasure that she'd taken the initiative.

"Trinity." No hello, just her name. "I need your help."

His help? Panic hit him. Was she in trouble?

"Anything." There were few things he wouldn't do for this woman.

She told him what she needed and he burst into laughter.

"Okay, princess, I have everything you need. I'll save your royal hind end."

* * *

From the corner of her eye Trinity watched Riley trail a long curly ribbon across the floor, enticing Casper to pounce, which the cat quickly did, only to have Riley tug the string a little further away.

"She'll never tire of that, you know," she warned, liking it that he was a cat kind of man. That he hadn't minded that she'd brought Casper with her. Chase had been more into dogs. She liked both. "She likes to play."

"Smart cat." He dangled the ribbon out in front of the cat, causing Casper to swat at a curl.

"Because she likes to play?"

"Every good girl should take time to play."

"That a dig at me?"

"No, ma'am, but if the shoe fits."

If the shoe fit? Ha, if he only knew that Jewel was hoping he'd shove her feet into a pair of glass slippers he wouldn't be making jokes about shoes fitting.

He nodded then glanced at where she was attempting to fold wrapping paper around a box. "Are you sure you don't want me to do that for you?"

"I can wrap a present."

His gaze dropped to the box and he scratched his head. "I'm sure you can, but maybe I could help you. It's not a crime to accept help from time to time."

She glanced down at the bunched-up paper and then at the previous package she'd wrapped. "They certainly don't look like the ones in the store," she mused, casting a longing eye at his perfectly wrapped present then onward to his Christmas tree. "Or the ones under your tree."

"They don't have to look any certain way," he assured her, helping her straighten the wrapping. He gently pushed Casper out of the way when the cat attempted to pounce on the paper, obviously not finished with having Riley's attention. Her cat really was smart. Brilliant, even.

"It's not the packaging that matters, Trinity," he continued, smoothing the paper Casper had managed to crinkle. "Like a lot of things in life, it's what's inside that counts."

"Yeah, well, I'm not sure about what's inside either." She gave the packages a skeptical look, handed him the string so he could occupy her cat while she attempted to wrap presentable gifts. "It wasn't easy buying something for someone I've never met."

"You did fine. My mom will love her gift and that you brought her something. She loves presents." He tugged on the string again, sending Casper into another pouncing fit. "For that matter, she's going to love you."

"Let's hope so."

She was nervous about meeting his family, wanted them to like her, had gone out on the worst evening to Christmas shop and fought the crowds to buy them gifts. She'd even picked up little gifts for his nieces and nephews. Her, Christmas shopping. Whatever had come over her?

And then there was Riley's gift. Something silly and ridiculous and so emotionally expensive she hadn't been sure she could pay the price. Yet the moment the idea had struck her, she'd known that's what she wanted to give him.

Something she hoped would have meaning to him and make him smile.

She pulled off a piece of tape and stuck it to the box she was working on. She managed to get all the box covered with paper, but she used a lot of tape in the process. At the rate she was going, they'd have to make a tape run soon.

Much to Casper's delight, Riley tossed the curled string of ribbon onto the floor. Grinning, he scooted over beside her and cut a new sheet of the wrapping paper the stores she'd been at had sold out of. Thank goodness, he'd been more than willing to not only share, but to help out with all the other things she hadn't even thought of asking him if he'd had, such as tape, name tags, and ribbons.

"Here." He set another box in the center of the cut paper. He placed his hands on her face and forced her to look at him. "Let me show you how I do this then you can develop your own technique."

Trying to ignore the bolts of electricity zooming through her at his touch, she grimaced at the roughly wrapped package sitting beside her. "I certainly need to lose my current technique. I'm horrible at wrapping."

At lots of things. Things she wanted to be good at. To be mind-blowing at.

"You just need a little guidance and then some practice." He stroked his thumb across her cheek. "I'm more than happy to oblige."

"Is sex that way, too?"

That had his eyes bulging and her grimacing.

"What do you mean?"

Her and her big mouth. Why had she had to say anything? Then again, she really did want to know. Because she thought about sex with this man a lot. Sometimes in a good fantasy way and others as in a scary way that would have him changing his phone number and running when he spotted her in the hospital hallways.

"I told you I'm horrible at that, too," she admitted, wondering if she was like the worst woman ever in making her admission. Then again, if she'd thought she could fake it successfully, they'd have gotten naked on the beach the night he'd cooked for her. She'd wanted to but had been scared of losing him, something she hadn't been ready to admit, much less risk. "Is sex something you'd instruct me in and then help me practice?"

"Princess, happy doesn't begin to convey how I feel about helping you with sex, but I've kissed you and know how wonderfully sensual you are. My guess is that you're better than you think."

If only. She knew she wasn't. She'd been there. And if she hadn't been, well, Chase had told her and the entire Christmas party how awful she'd been in the sack.

"No, I'm not."

Twisting a piece of ribbon around the package, he frowned. "Not that I believe for one minute that it's true, but what makes you say that you're not any good at sex? Are you a virgin?"

"No," she said quickly. Did he think she'd just made up that she lacked bedroom skills? That wasn't exactly the kind of thing a woman went around tooting her horn about. At least, none she'd ever known. "My ex told me how terrible I am."

"Your ex was an idiot." His words were immediate and matter-of-fact.

"Well, yes, he was." Chase had been. She could see that now. "But, unfortunately, on that matter, he was right. I didn't enjoy sex and won't be winning any Oscars for my bedroom performance."

"If you didn't enjoy sex, then he was the one who was lacking, not you." Riley's gaze bored into her, making

her want to squirm. "It's his job to see to it you're enjoying sex, Trinity. If you weren't and he blamed you,
he was an even bigger idiot than I thought."

Than he thought? She'd barely mentioned Chase to
him, because mentioning her ex just brought her down,
made her worry that Riley would move on as well. Riley
was so much more than Chase had ever been. Why
wouldn't he move on?

"What do you know about Chase?"

For once, it was he who averted his gaze and started
wrapping the present, but as if he realized what he'd
done and didn't like the action, he met her gaze head
on. "Just what little you've told me…and what I overheard you tell Jewel Hendrix."

"You were listening to my conversation?" Her cheeks
heated. That would teach her to have inappropriate conversations with older women who went on and on about
glass slippers and Prince Charming.

"Perhaps I shouldn't have, but I did."

She digested that, trying to recall just what all she
and Jewel had said about Chase…and Riley himself.
"What else did you overhear?"

"That he dumped you at a hospital Christmas party.
Sounds like a jerk."

"He did and he was."

"He didn't deserve you," Riley said immediately,
with such conviction that she had to stare at him in wonder. He believed that. He believed in her. The question
was, could she believe in him?

"No, he didn't." Warmth lit inside her and spread
through her chest. "Funny that it's taken me two years
to realize that."

Riley paused from wrapping the present to take her

hand and kiss her fingers. "Is he why you don't like Christmas?"

"Partly."

"And the other part is the lack of Christmas while growing up?"

She wasn't sure she liked him knowing so much about her, the real her beneath the surface. Riley and Jewel had a lot in common.

"Not in the way you probably mean," she admitted softly, wishing they could just not have this conversation.

"Which is?"

"It's not that I expected grand presents or anything, it just would have been nice to have had a little bit of normalcy during my childhood."

Wow. She couldn't believe she was saying the words out loud, that she was admitting that her life wasn't perfect, because to make that admission just begged for someone to want to dig deeper.

For Riley to dig deeper.

She knew he would. So why hadn't she shut this conversation down? Instead, if anything, she'd encouraged it.

His hold on her hand tightened then he let go, started working on the present again. "By normalcy, you mean like a Norman Rockwell painting?"

"Not really." Normalcy, as in a Norman Rockwell painting? As in a mother and a father making a big deal over her, over having a brother or a sister to squabble with over who got to open the first gift. She hadn't ever really thought of normalcy that way, but perhaps, if she had, that's exactly how she would have envisioned an ideal childhood Christmas. "Maybe."

"I should warn you, my family is very non-normal. Christmas with us is more along the lines of a mad-house. The whole bunch are touched in the head."

She could hear the love in his voice and was honestly more than a little jealous. "Must run in the family."

"Must do," he agreed, holding up the wrapped gift for her inspection. *"Voilà!"*

"Nice." Every angle was perfectly aligned and taped down. "Do I have to be a heart surgeon to achieve something similar?"

"Nope, just need a little patience and a whole lot of practice. Here." He cut off a piece of paper and flattened it out on the floor, then placed the box in the middle. "Your turn."

Trinity wrapped the remainder of her presents with Riley's help. The packages weren't as neat as the one he'd done alone, but by the last one she was impressed with the progress she'd made.

"Look!" she exclaimed as she ran the edge of the scissors over the length of ribbon, causing a perfect curl to form. "I did it!"

His eyes were warm, full of praise. "I knew you could."

His faith in her was so evident, so real as to almost be palpable. "You did, didn't you?"

"It was a no-brainer."

When no one her entire life had believed in her, why did he? What did he see that no one else did? "Why's that?"

"You're a smart woman who can do anything you set your mind to."

"Thank you, but you're giving me more credit than I deserve."

"I don't think so. I just think you don't give yourself enough credit. Not where a lot of things are concerned. You really are the most amazing woman, Trinity."

Not knowing what to say to his comment, she made a show of surveying the assembly of presents. "I hope they like them."

His gaze stayed on her rather than the presents. "They will. They aren't picky. They're used to dealing with me, remember?"

He was so close to perfect it wasn't real. His family would see right away that they were from two different ends of the spectrum. A bubble of panic rose in her throat.

"What if they don't like me?"

"They will like you. Weren't you paying attention? They aren't picky." He grinned while he said the last and she knew he was attempting to ease her concerns. His easy smile and confidence did go a long way to dismantling her anxiety. The man's constant good humor was contagious.

She slapped his arm playfully. He had such a way of making her feel better. "Shame on you, Riley."

His eyes twinkled with merriment. "For?"

"Teasing me when I'm nervous about meeting your family."

"No worries, princess. I know they are going to love you. Besides, turnabout is fair play and you can tease me when I meet your family."

Which was yet another reason why she should have shut this conversation down a long time ago. She bit the inside of her bottom lip. "Won't happen."

His brow rose. "You don't plan to keep me around

long enough to have need to introduce me to your family?"

His tone was teasing, but a real question shone in his eyes.

"It's not that. We both know you'll be the one to get bored with me and walk away. Not vice versa." She hated the thought of him doing so. If she'd felt a panic bubble before, she felt a panic volcano now. "If you think back, I told you that I don't know my father, and my mother died a few years ago." Right before she'd started dating Chase, actually. "There's no family for me to introduce you to."

"No uncles or aunts or cousins?"

If there were she'd never met or heard of any of them. She shook her head.

"Oh, princess, that's terrible. Come here." He wrapped his arms around her and hugged her close, much as a parent would a child.

Trinity couldn't say her lack of family was terrible, just her reality, but Riley's arms around her felt good so she wasn't going to argue with him. Instead, she snuggled against him and rested her cheek against the hard plane of his chest, soaking in his strength.

"I'm sorry, honey. I didn't know."

"It's okay." How could he have known? How could anyone have known when she kept all her emotions bottled up inside her? Even now she wondered if she'd made a mistake, letting him know so much. "Does it matter?"

He pulled back to stare down at her. "Of course it matters. Family is one's support system and you've had to face life without that."

Her mother had been her only family and, honestly,

she hadn't been supportive, at least, not that Trinity could recall. More that Trinity had been an unexpected nuisance that had come along and interrupted her buzz.

"Not all families are supportive."

"True, and there are times mine drive me crazy, but I wouldn't trade them for the world." He kissed the top of her head. "Well, you'll see what I mean after you meet them tomorrow."

With that, a renewed dread of meeting his family, of having to endure a Christmas dinner and be smacked in the face with what all she didn't have in her life hit her. A renewed fear of what this Christmas Day would bring because, seriously, Christmas was never good for her. "You're really going to make me go?"

"You know I am. You gave me your word."

She nodded. She'd expected no less. "What should I wear?"

"Clothes. If you don't, my mother will be highly upset with me," he said with a deadpan expression that was unlike him.

"Okay, smartypants, what kind of clothes? A dress or just something casual?"

He grinned and she realized he'd once again purposely tried to distract her. "Casual. There's a lot of us, and I do mean a lot, and we're very informal. Just dress in whatever you're going to be most comfortable in."

"Okay." She leaned her head against him, drawing on his strength yet again and hoping she didn't disappoint him. "Thank you, Riley."

"For teaching you to wrap presents?"

"That, too, but I meant for just being here with me, period."

"With you is where I want to be. I was a bit lost with-

out you tonight. I've gotten quite accustomed to eating dinner with you and hanging out afterwards. Being
without you left me at a loose end and I didn't like it."

"I feel the same."

He tilted her chin to where she had to face him.
"You do?"

With everything else she'd already told him, what
was one more admission? "I think about you from the
time I wake up until the time I go to sleep and all the
time in between."

Okay, so maybe that had been a big admission.

"And your dreams? Am I there, too?" He spoke so
close to her mouth that she could feel the warm mois-
ture in his breath.

Her own breath caught, held, and blew out in an excited little burst of anticipation of his lips touching hers.
He was going to kiss her. She knew he was. She wanted
him to. Needed him to.

"Oh, yes, Riley, you are in my dreams." She low-
ered her lids then met his gaze head on, not trying to
hide what she knew was in her eyes. "You and moun-
tains of mistletoe."

CHAPTER ELEVEN

THINKING HIMSELF THE luckiest man alive, Riley accepted the invitation she'd just tossed out. He wanted to kiss her more than he wanted his next breath.

Her lips were hot and met his with a hunger that surprised him.

A hunger that matched his own.

His hands were in her hair.

Her hands were in his hair.

Threading through the locks, pulling him to her, grasping tightly as if she never wanted to let go.

His mouth left the lushness of her lips to travel down her throat, to sup at the graceful arch of her neck. She smelled of heaven, she tasted even sweeter.

Her hands had gone to his waist, were running over his lower back, pulling him towards her with an urgency that had his head spinning.

He groaned. He wanted her more than he'd thought it possible to want someone. He wanted her to the point his body ached with need, but more than that his mind craved her. Craved knowing what she looked like with pleasure on her face, craved knowing how she sounded when she experienced full and total release, craved the knowledge that he'd put that look on her face, made that sound escape her perfect plump lips.

He kissed and supped and touched.

She rubbed and massaged and arched against him, exposing the beauty of her neck more fully. He took full advantage, moving lower and lower.

He didn't consciously consider cupping her breasts, but his hands did so as if they had a mind of their own and had taken charge. No wonder. Her breasts were amazing and made him want her all the more, which he'd have thought impossible as he already wanted so much.

"That feels good."

Had she said the words or him?

His mouth must have developed an agenda of its own, too, because when his hands pushed away her top and bra, his lips covered the perfection of her creamy breast. His gut clenched.

He'd changed into jeans when he'd arrived home. Now he longed for the comfort of his loose slacks because his jeans had grown way too snug.

As if she'd read his mind, Trinity's fingers undid his jeans and slid beneath the material of his shirt. She ran her fingers along his abs, tracing lightly but with the effect of lightning bolts, before moaning and pulling him close enough that their bodies molded together.

"More," she demanded, her fingers going into his hair and pulling his mouth to hers. The moment his mouth covered hers, they both began to make haste with his shirt buttons, with her pushed-aside shirt, until they both stood bare chested against each other.

More sounded just about right. He wanted more. Lots more.

* * *

Somewhere in the recesses of her mind a small voice warned Trinity that she needed to stop. Sure, everything was going just fine at the moment but she really wasn't any good at this. If she didn't stop, Riley was soon going to discover that fact for himself, and then what?

But her body wasn't listening to her brain. Her body was way too busy discovering new and wonderful sensations that his mouth and hands were distributing all the way through her.

In a minute she'd stop, but for now she just wanted to feel everything he so generously gave. Surely that wasn't so wrong? After all, it was Christmas Eve.

So rather than cover her breasts when her shirt fell to the floor, she dropped her head back and basked in the absolute glory of his eyes feasting on her. They did. As if her body was the most beautiful thing he'd ever seen. Wow. How did he do that? Make her feel so good without saying a word?

So when his hands and mouth returned to work, she wasn't surprised that the rest of her body wanted to get closer, to get in on the action. Her hips ground against him, marveling at the hardness pressing against her, marveling at how he breathed raggedly, at how absolutely turned on he was. By her.

His hands sliding her pants down her hips felt natural, like the most perfect thing ever. Standing before him, his eyes eating up the image of her in only her peach-colored panties could never be wrong as long as he looked at her with that light in his eyes. He wanted her. More than she'd ever been wanted, Riley wanted her. Being the object of his desire was a heady high.

One that left her wanting more. And more. And more.

Unable to stand still another moment, she moved to him, kissed him, ran her fingers over the beauty of his shoulders, his chest.

Strong, chiseled, the way a man's body should look. He was so beautiful. So much so she should probably feel intimidated, but how could she when he was so obviously affected by her, when his eyes had been soaking up the sight of her body like a starved man? When he now touched her with that same urgency?

The open snap of his jeans dug into her belly, reminding her they were in her way. She slid her hands down over the hard planes of his abdominal muscles and into the edges of his waistband. She gave a hard tug. His hands immediately joined hers in removing his clothes.

Then they stood in front of each other, he in navy boxer briefs, she in panties that were growing more and more damp.

"You're beautiful."

She shook her head. "You are."

He smiled.

She smiled back and nodded. She knew better than to do this. Especially at Christmas, but she wasn't stopping.

Trinity sighed with contentment in her sleep, rousing herself. Without opening her eyes, she smiled.

Really, really smiled.

Because Riley had been right. Chase had been wrong. She hadn't been horrible at sex. She'd just been having sex with the wrong man.

And Riley was the right man.

A bubble of panic flitted through her, but her body glowed with contentment and her joy was too great to let doubt take hold. Not now. Now she wanted what she hadn't had the first time she'd woken up with Riley. She wanted to wake him up with kisses, make him smile.

Then, she hadn't believed herself capable. Now, she knew better. He'd woken a siren within her. And not one who was horrible either.

Smiling, she rolled over, only to come shockingly fully awake.

She was alone.

Alone.

She reached out and touched where Riley had been in the bed beside her, her hand running over the cool sheet. Apparently he'd been gone for some time. Was he in the other room? Or perhaps out on the deck? Regardless, he wasn't in this bed next to her.

Where she wanted him to be. Where he should be.

Her heart twisted in grief. Had she been wrong? No, he had enjoyed the sex as much as she had. She knew he had. She might not be the best he'd ever had, but she had given him pleasure. A lot of pleasure.

But maybe sex was all he'd wanted from her and now that he'd gotten it, he was done. Perhaps having left her in his bed was his way of telling her not to get too attached, that they wouldn't be waking up in each other's arms.

Really, she'd known better. Had known that when she'd had sex everything would come to a screeching halt. She hadn't needed it to be Christmas to achieve that feat, but she doubted the day of the year had helped any.

Would she never learn?

Recalling all the touches she and Riley had shared, the way their bodies had melted as if made to fit together, the way she'd seen stars flash in front of her eyes and cried out his name, the way he'd growled hers in a torrent of release, she couldn't regret the night before. Whatever Riley's reasons for not being in this bed, it wasn't that she had been horrible in bed and for him giving her that knowledge, freeing her from that burden Chase had saddled her with, for that she was grateful. Not only had he shown her otherwise, he'd given her the greatest experience she'd ever known.

Not just the sex, though. Every moment in his company was precious. He was precious.

She loved him.

Despite all the reasons she knew better, she loved Riley Williams.

She should leave. She should go let her cat out of his guest bathroom and she should leave.

Instead, she closed her eyes and pulled the pillow that his head had once rested on over her head, cursing her stupidity for falling in love with a man who was so far out of her league and who could never really be her Prince Charming, even if he did call her princess.

Had the past taught her nothing?

The tears that burned her eyes were nowhere near as hot as the ones that seared her heart.

His mind racing, Riley carried the last box of his supplies into Trinity's apartment. He hit the front door with his hip, wincing when it closed a little more loudly than he'd intended.

No one might be home but he didn't want any of her neighbors calling the law on him either. Then again, maybe they'd just think it was Santa making all the noise. He felt like Santa.

He'd worried how he would be able to pull off her Christmas gift without her knowing what he was up to. Leaving her warm, sexy body naked in his bed hadn't been easy, but her surprise would be worth it.

He couldn't suppress the grin on his face.

He'd promised Trinity the best Christmas ever and he was going to deliver.

She'd already given him the best Christmas ever.

The best night ever.

The best everything ever.

She'd rocked his world. In so many ways. Trinity had certainly knocked him for a loop. A good one. Like a carnival ride that thrilled and made you want to just keep coming back for more.

He glanced around her living room, smiling at his efforts. What would she think?

She professed to not like Christmas, but he'd never seen anyone more starved for the magic of the holidays. He wanted to give her that magic. He wanted to make all her dreams come true.

To make her day feel as if she lived a fairy-tale. He wanted to make every day of her life feel like a fairy-tale.

Which struck him as odd. His thoughts were those of happy-ever-after, not those of a man who knew he couldn't do to a woman what his father had done to his mother. Yet he couldn't bring himself to think of a future without Trinity.

Because he loved her.

Oh, hell.

He couldn't love her.

But he did.

Yet what kind of Prince Charming could he be when he'd forever be called away from her for his career?

With shaky hands and a heavy heart he finished what he'd snuck her keys out of her purse and driven to her apartment to do.

No Prince Charming had ever done better.

Too bad he was a Prince Charming who couldn't give a happy-ever-after.

Maybe if she didn't open her eyes, she could just pretend she wasn't awake and could sleep straight through Christmas. Darn whoever had changed the schedule at work and left her home alone today.

Only she wasn't at home.

She was at Riley's. In his bed. Alone.

She tugged on the covers, trying to pull them over her head, but they wouldn't budge. Which had her eyes popping open to see why.

"Good morning, princess."

"But…" She stared in shock at the man sitting at the foot of the bed, looking sexy as all get-out with only his jeans on. Wow. Maybe she *was* dreaming.

She stared at him, trying to reconcile the fact that he was here, that he was smiling and teasing her. Had she dreamed waking up in his bed alone? Dozens of conflicting emotions swirled inside her.

Last night had hurt. A lot. But he hadn't left because he was right here in front of her.

Of course he hadn't left. She'd been in his bed, in his house.

"Why?"

He looked confused. "Why what?"

"Why are you here?"

His brow arched. "Is that a trick question? I live here." His expression darkened. "Don't you want me here?"

How did she answer that? Did you tell a man that you'd woken up and found the bed empty and had assumed the worst? That you'd cried yourself to sleep and erected a hundred new walls to replace the ones he'd torn down because she'd realized she was in love with him?

"I woke up and you weren't here." Did she sound whiny?

She'd thought he would take a hint and tell her why he'd left his bed, but he just shrugged, as if his absence was no big deal. Only he didn't meet her eyes and he wasn't smiling.

"Sometimes a man has to do what a man has to do. Now, out of bed. Time's awasting."

He might convince her to get out of bed except there was an itsy bitsy tiny problem. "I'm naked."

"Good point." His smile was lethal and he suddenly seemed intent on lightening the mood between them. "Forget getting out of bed. I'll get back in with you. Much better idea." With that he dove towards her, tugging on the covers she had tucked beneath her chin.

"No." She wiggled and squirmed, trying to prevent him from uncovering her body. "No, I don't want you to see me like this."

He stilled. "Like this? I saw everything there was to see about your body last night. Up close and personal from all angles. Have your forgotten?"

"No, but…" How did she explain that when she'd woken and he hadn't been there she'd felt such devastation and had grieved and erected those walls to where she just didn't trust letting them back down. She didn't want to let them back down. Right or wrong since he obviously hadn't really left, she still felt defensive.

Or perhaps it was her other realization during the night that had her so defensive. She didn't want to be in love with him.

"Riley, I don't want to do this today."

"This?"

"You know."

He blinked and tugged at the covers again.

Holding them tight, she shook her head. "No."

He let go of the comforter. "What are you saying?"

Her grip on the comforter tightened. "Last night shouldn't have happened."

"Because?"

What could she say? That she was so damaged by her past that she couldn't bear any more pain? That she'd fallen in love with him and although she'd thought she was strong enough to be with him and survive when he got bored with her crazy hang-ups, last night had shown her otherwise?

"Fine," he agreed between gritted teeth. "Last night was a mistake."

She couldn't tell if he was being sarcastic or angry.

"At least get out of bed and come and see what Santa left you."

Her heart dropped somewhere to the pit of her stomach. "Please, don't."

Because she just couldn't take such comments this morning. She just couldn't pretend she was the same as him, that she could spend the night in his bed and go and be all jolly with his family. She couldn't pretend that she didn't love him and that she was terrified of that realization.

"Don't?" He raked his fingers through his hair then scooted up beside her, gently forced her to look at him. "Talk to me, Trinity. I thought you'd wake up smiling this morning, not looking at me as if I'm the Grinch who stole Christmas."

"No, that would be me. I'm the one who dislikes Christmas, remember?"

"That's just because you're so stubborn and refuse to give Christmas a chance. Quit being otherwise, get out of bed, and let's enjoy our Christmas morning together before it's time to leave for my mom's. We'll discuss last night some other time, but for now I promised you the best Christmas ever. Accomplishing that does require some effort on your part."

A sick feeling settled in her stomach. "What have you done?"

Because she didn't want him going and setting a precedent that every other year would have to live up to and never would. She didn't want him being nice to her because he felt sorry for her that her mother just hadn't been into Christmas. That Chase had messed with her head and heart. She didn't want to be another of Riley's charity cases.

"I didn't say I did anything. But maybe you were a very good girl this year, and Santa came to see you last night."

She didn't want him making her depend on him even more than she already did. That was becoming more and more difficult each day and after last night... She shook her head. He probably thought her a charity case all the way round. Maybe that's what the past few weeks had been about. She was this year's Christmas project. "No, whatever it is you've done, just undo it."

His jaw tightened. "You want me to undo your Christmas morning?"

She nodded. "I don't want you being nice to me."

"Now I'm really confused."

"Don't you see?" She fought sniffling. "You've got to stop doing this."

His eyes filled with concern. "I don't see at all. You've stumped me. What exactly do I have to stop doing?"

"Making me want to believe."

He reached over, ran his finger across her face and tucked a hair behind her ear. "Now, why would I want you to stop believing when the whole idea is to make you believe in Christmas?"

Only she hadn't been talking about Christmas.

She'd been referring to him.

CHAPTER TWELVE

RILEY SCRATCHED HIS head in total confusion while Trinity got out of the bed without his assistance and with the comforter wrapped around her delectable body. He'd have liked to have woken her up with kisses, but he hadn't wanted her to get the wrong idea.

Which meant there was a right idea.

He wasn't exactly sure what that was, but he figured he had some time to figure it out. To figure them out because he wasn't a forever kind of man and she deserved her own happy-ever-after.

At least he'd thought he had time and had told himself he just wouldn't think about the future today, that he'd focus on the holiday and giving Trinity a day to remember always.

He just didn't understand why she'd be back to bah-humbugging after the night they'd shared. He'd thought the night amazing, had expected all smiles and happiness on his favorite day of the year. Instead, she'd seemed determined to be contrary. Did she want to ruin their day? To fight?

Frowning, he slipped his shirt from the night before back on and went into his living room, surveying the room and trying to see it as she would.

He hadn't gone overboard at his house, just hung on his fireplace mantel a stocking with her name in glitter on it. Plus a few presents. He'd wanted her main gift to be a complete surprise. Had he not done a little something for her, she'd definitely have suspected.

He wanted to catch her off guard and blow her mind.

"Riley?"

He hadn't heard her step up behind him.

"What is all this?"

She'd put on one of his T-shirts and a drawstring pair of shorts that came down past her knees. She'd combed her hair and tied it back with a rubber band. Her face was freshly washed and ethereally beautiful. She looked like an angel.

One he was now afraid to touch for fear of upsetting her further. For fear that his feelings might show and set up expectations he couldn't follow through on.

"Christmas morning."

She glanced around the room, taking in where he had their breakfast cooked and waiting on the table, taking in the small package sitting beside her plate, taking in all the details of the room but not smiling. Instead, she looked distraught. "Why?"

He could list any number of reasons and all of them rang with truth. The panicky paleness to her face warned he might have miscalculated who she really was. "Because I want to make you happy."

But had obviously failed miserably.

Her face pinched with obvious disappointment. "You think you have to give me things to do that?"

"No." He frowned. She was taking all his efforts the wrong way. Not at all how he'd envisioned. "Haven't you ever heard it's more blessed to give than to receive?"

Without saying anything, she walked over to the fireplace mantel, ran her finger over the red velvet stocking with her name on it.

"There are presents inside."

She glanced down at the bulges in the stocking. Her face was still pinched. "I see that."

"They're yours." He'd wanted to watch her tear into the presents with excited gusto, wanted joy to sparkle on her face and laughter to curve her lips. He'd wanted her to throw her arms around him and wish him a merry Christmas. Instead, she appeared to be somewhere between starting to cry and darting out of the room.

"I…I'm not sure."

She didn't intend to open his gifts? What the…? He sucked in a deep breath. "Fine. If you don't want to open your presents, we can eat breakfast first."

"I'm not really hungry."

Determined that he was somehow going to lighten her mood without letting her ruin his, he waggled his brows. "If you don't want to open presents and you aren't hungry, then whatever do we do to pass the time until we go to my mom's house?"

Her gaze narrowed. "Not what you're thinking."

Yeah, her "Last night was a mistake" had clued him in that she wouldn't be dangling any mistletoe over her head any time soon. He crossed his arms. "You don't know what I'm thinking."

"Sure, I do."

"Then you should be ashamed of yourself."

She didn't crack a smile.

"Come on, Trinity. Lighten up. It's Christmas and

we're young and healthy and have a lot of things to be thankful for. I've done my best to give you a special Christmas morning. Why are you acting this way?"

Trinity felt like a grade-A heel. She was being an ungrateful pain when he was doing his best to make the most of the morning. She realized that.

Just as she realized that she wanted to give in to his cajoling. But what would be the point?

Last night had blown her away then blown her to bits.

She was in love with him. Just look at how she'd fallen apart when she and Chase had ended. Chase had been nothing compared to Riley.

Nothing.

She'd given her word she'd go with him today, but beyond that she couldn't do more. Couldn't risk more.

He was a good man. He deserved more. Deserved better than she could ever be.

He deserved someone who could look around at the effort he'd made to make her Christmas morning special and express her appreciation, not clam up with fear and panic. Someone who could give him good things in return.

Casper mewed at her feet and she bent over to pick up the cat, stroking the silky fur.

"I fed her some tuna. Hope that's okay and that I didn't do something else wrong."

Ouch. Usually he was so patient, but he must have reached his limit. She couldn't fault him for that.

Walking over to the table where he'd prepared a small feast, she sat in a chair, putting Casper in her lap. The cat nuzzled her a brief moment then jumped down to rub against Riley's leg. She didn't blame her cat. She'd choose rubbing against Riley's leg over her lap, too.

She and her cat could mope over him together when he was gone.

Her gaze fell on the brightly wrapped present next to her plate. "I don't have your present with me."

"You got me a present?"

Embarrassed, she nodded. "It's not anything big. Just a little something that you will probably think silly."

"Not a problem. We'll go by your place on the way to my mother's. I figure you will need to shower and change anyway."

"Actually, I have a bag in my car and could grab a quick shower here if that's okay." Because if she went home, he might not prise her back outside the door to go to his mother's. She might be a coward, but she wasn't a liar. She'd told him she'd go, so she would go. If he still wanted her to. "I keep a change of clothes in my car because of never knowing when I'm going to get off work."

"Whatever is fine. Can I get it for you?"

She shook her head. "Sit down. You've obviously worked hard this morning getting all this together. The least I can do is co-operate."

She could tell he was disappointed. By her words and her actions.

She just wanted this day over.

"Will you please open your presents?"

Glancing at the package, she nodded. Really, how could she say no?

With shaky hands she unwrapped the present, her breath catching at what was inside. An angel tree-topper.

"Thank you." She didn't point out that she didn't have a tree.

"You're welcome." He sounded as awkward as she did.

That the packages inside her stocking contained various Christmas ornaments didn't surprise her. Not really. What an optimist he was.

Part of her knew she'd treasure the gifts always. Another part wondered if she'd ever be able to look at them without remembering that the day he'd given them to her had been the beginning of the end.

Apparently, he was going to fail at giving Trinity a magical day. Not that he wasn't trying, but he could only do so much when she wouldn't look him in the eye and even her smile was fake.

Maybe he should have just taken her home instead of torturing himself with failure for the remainder of the day.

He didn't deal well with failure.

Especially when he didn't know why he was failing. He loved this woman and wanted to make her day special. Why was everything coming out wrong?

Because he was the wrong Prince Charming?

"You can take me home if you've changed your mind about wanting me with you today."

"Hell, no," he snapped, knowing he sounded harsh, but seriously, if that was her game and she'd purposely been aloof all morning to get out of spending Christmas with him, she could think again.

"Fine, but just remember that I did offer."

He tried to hold her hand as they walked around the car, but she pulled away under the pretense of helping him carry packages. He frowned but figured that her refusing to hold his hand was par for the course today.

Fine. She could act all weird if that's what she wanted, but today was Christmas and he was going to enjoy the day if it killed him.

His mother's house was in chaos as usual, being Christmas Day. There were easily more than thirty people present. They all looked to be having a great time and happy to be there. Except Trinity didn't want to be there and was doing a poor job of hiding that fact. Several times on the trip from the car to the house he'd thought she might make a run for it.

"Please, don't make me do this."

Frustrated beyond belief, he stopped walking to glare at her. "You act as if being here is making you a martyr."

She winced. "I'm sorry. It's just that I—"

"Uncle Riley is here!" Timmy, his sister's oldest, screamed, and came racing toward him. The seven-year-old launched himself at Riley, cutting off whatever Trinity had been going to say. "Did you bring presents?"

"Have I ever come to Christmas without presents?" he snapped, and regretted it even before Timmy's face fell. "Sorry, bud," he apologized to his favorite nephew, who stared at him as if aliens must have invaded his body. Riley sighed, gave the kid a hug, then sat him down on the pavement. "There are more in the car if you want to round up a posse to help unload."

Still looking at him as if trying to figure out what was up, Timmy and several of his other nephews, who seemed to appear out of thin air, ran towards his car.

Setting down the presents that he held, he turned

to face Trinity. "I know you don't want to be here, but Christmas is special to my family and I don't want the day ruined for my mother. She's been through a lot. Try to at least pretend you want to be here with me, okay?"

Looking pale, Trinity just nodded and was then overwhelmed by his mother and sisters. Being cornered by the Williams women could be compared to nothing less than an all-out assault.

"Oh, look at you, honey. What a pretty little thing you are!" his mother said, her hands on Trinity's shoulders as she studied her.

"Mom, you're embarrassing her," said Riley's younger sister, who then proceeded to do the same but pulled Trinity into a hug that she remained stiff through.

"Nah," said his sister, who was currently eight months pregnant and looked as if she was about to pop. "All women like to be called pretty and little."

"Hey, pretty little sister," Riley greeted her, stressing *pretty* and *little*. He kissed her cheek. "Mom, Becky, this is Trinity. We work together at the hospital."

Because what more could he say?

"You more than work together or she wouldn't be here with you." That had come from his brother, who'd joined them and slapped Riley across the shoulder.

Riley wanted to laugh, to shake his brother's hand and make a joke of his comment, but instead he just shrugged. "It's no big deal, really."

"Right," his older sister said, wrapping her arms around him and kissing his cheek. "Great to see you, little brother. And Trinity." She turned to a pale Trinity and did the same. "We're so glad that Riley has finally brought a woman home with him. We've all been placing bets as to what you looked like."

"Bets?" Trinity's eyes resembled those of a doe in headlights. Her skin was pasty white and her posture stiff as a board.

Riley winced. "Sis, you're scaring her."

"Nah, if she's with you, she isn't easily scared."

His siblings all burst into laughter but Trinity remained quiet, and regret filled Riley. He'd made a mistake, bringing her here.

After the disaster of a morning they'd had, maybe he should just admit that everything about them was a mistake. He couldn't give her what she deserved and she didn't want anything he tried to give.

Maybe she really didn't like Christmas.

Or him.

Ending things as soon as possible was inevitable.

Trinity had made a mistake in coming here with Riley. Seriously, she should just hibernate through Christmas each year. She'd be a happier person if she did.

Those around her would be happier because she knew she was ruining Riley's day and that was a shame, but she felt unable to snap out of her melancholy.

She'd had sex with him the night before. Amazing, beautiful sex where they'd not held anything back from each other. Today she could barely look at him for the panic filling her mind.

Would he dump her on Christmas, as Chase had? Perhaps publicly do so in front of his family? His affluent family? She might not know the actual values of cars but the cars in Riley's mother's drive weren't at the low end of the market.

They couldn't be more different.

They'd probably all lost their bets because she

doubted any of them had bet on Riley bringing a charity case.

"Jake here thought you'd be tall and a buxomy redhead." A woman who looked a lot like Riley clarified her earlier comment, oblivious to Trinity's inner torment. "I thought you'd be tall, thin and blonde. Becky thought you'd be brunette."

"And I thought you'd be the luckiest girl in the world to be here with my wonderful son," Riley's mom butted in, shooing them all further into the house. "Come on in so we can say a blessing for our meal." The kids came running through with more packages. "Boys, y'all put those under the tree for now. We'll open presents after we all have full bellies."

"But, Nana!"

"Don't Nana me. You heard me." But her voice was full of love, rather than threat.

They were all being friendly, trying to include her, had smothered her with hugs and attention.

But Trinity felt the difference in Riley and knew she had no one to blame but herself. She'd known better than to come here, to become involved with him from the very beginning, and yet she had.

Because she had felt something when she'd looked at him that she hadn't been able to resist and she'd made the mistake of falling in love with a man she could never have.

"Don't pay them any mind." A very tanned, very blonde woman who looked like she'd stepped off a vacation ad for Florida advised her. "The whole Williams clan are nothing but troublemakers."

Trinity just blinked at the gorgeous woman.

"Hi, I'm Casey, Jake's wife. You must be Trinity.

Come and sit by me. I'll protect you from the Williamses."

"Hello," Riley interrupted with a scowl, stopping Casey from taking Trinity's arm. "In case you've forgotten, you are one of us Williamses now, too."

The woman flashed pearly-white teeth that contrasted brightly with her tanned skin. "Happiest day of my life."

Jake wrapped his arm around her waist and planted a kiss on the woman's mouth right there and didn't stop with just a quick peck either.

Blushing, Trinity glanced around, but no one was paying the couple any heed. Apparently showing affection was the norm at the Williamses' house. No mistletoe required.

"Uncle Riley, will you sit with us?" the little boy Riley had called Timmy asked, jumping up and down near Riley as if he had ants in his pants.

"At the kids' table?" Riley scratched his jaw. "Not this year, Timmy. I've brought a guest with me. She needs me at the adult table with her. I have to protect her from the big people."

Not hiding his disappointment, the boy gave Trinity a disgusted look. "She's just a girl, Uncle Riley."

"Just a girl, he says." Riley ruffled the boy's hair. "I'll have to remind you of that in a few years."

Trinity found herself watching Riley's family interact, watched the open affection, the laughter, the genuine gladness to be together, and she tried not to feel envious. She also tried not to feel guilty that Riley frowned more than smiled. She wasn't the only one who noticed and, unfortunately, various family members would shoot them curious looks from time to time, but no one asked what the problem was.

They had to be wondering, though. Why would he bring someone who so obviously didn't fit in with their wonderful lives? Why did it even matter? After all, she wouldn't be seeing these people ever again. Riley wouldn't want her to.

He'd given in to his nephew's repeated requests to come and check out the new video game Santa had brought him or he'd just given up completely on her. Either way, he'd disappeared some time ago, which was probably for the best because something his brother had said to him had made him almost growl earlier.

In a room full of people, yet oddly alone at an open archway leading into the foyer, she took a sip of hot cinnamon apple cider, liking the mix of sweet and tangy flavors and wishing it would settle her nerves.

Wishing her insides didn't twist, her mind didn't doubt, her stomach didn't roil. That she really was a part of this family and could go and play video games with Riley and the kids. Or even lounge comfortably with the crew that was settling in to watch a football game and talking back and forth about which team was going to win.

She wished she could be a glass-half-full kind of girl, rather than what stared back at her in the mirror. How did one go about changing one's reflection?

She rested her head on the archway and wished she could blend into this love-filled family.

"She doesn't seem to be having a very good time. Neither do you, for that matter."

Ouch. Was she supposed to have been able to over-hear Riley's youngest sister? The pregnant one. She couldn't remember her name. She'd met so many different people today. Easily more than forty, although it might as well have been hundreds for how they'd made her head spin.

"We are a bit much to take in," Riley said defensively. Trinity's heart lurched at his defense but then crumbled at his next statement. "But you're right. I shouldn't have brought her here today, but she doesn't have any family and I didn't want her to be alone. Not on Christmas Day." He paused and she couldn't hear what his sister said. "Maybe, but, regardless, I made a grave miscalculation where she was concerned. One I dearly regret."

He wished he hadn't brought her? Well, duh, of course he wished he hadn't brought her. She was ruining his day with his family. What a Christmas-killer she was.

Determined not to dampen his day or this lovely family's day any more than she already had, she forced a smile onto her face and joined the closest group of adults to her.

Somehow she'd fake her way through the rest of the day.

Christmas couldn't end soon enough. Was she doomed to feel this way for ever?

Taking a quick glance toward Trinity as he pulled the car out onto the highway, Riley sighed. "You're quiet."

She'd been quiet most of the day. With him, at any rate. When he'd come out from trying to make up to Timmy for snapping at the boy, Trinity had joined a group playing cards. She'd laughed and had seemed to enjoy herself. Except when he'd come near. Then the silent treatment had rolled in.

"Sometimes it's better to say nothing at all."

"Than to say something bad?" On the day after they'd first made love. Christmas morning. The entire day should have been filled with smiles and happiness. She'd clammed up and shut him out rather than embrace the goodness of what they could have shared on what was probably the only Christmas they'd spend together.

"You think I would say something bad?"

Why was it he stuck his foot in his mouth so easily where she was concerned? He loved her. He didn't want to pick a fight with her. Not really. Or maybe he did because he felt so frustrated by the whole situation. At this point he wasn't sure what he wanted.

"No, I don't think you would say anything bad. What I think is that you'd sit quietly and answer a thousand questions as politely and concisely as you possibly could then go right back to being quiet, as if you'd taken a vow of silence rather than make any effort to make conversation."

Her face flushed pink. "I made an effort to talk to your family."

Keeping his eyes on the road and one hand on the steering-wheel, he raked his other hand through his hair. "I wanted you to like my family. To not have to make an effort to talk to them, but for it to flow naturally. I wanted them to like you."

"I did like them."

He heard her swallow and figured he'd said too much. That he should have held in what he wanted, because what he wanted didn't seem to matter.

"Did they not like me?"

A damn of emotion broke loose within him and he failed to hold his irritation in.

"They knew something wasn't right between us. I finally brought a woman home and they all kept asking me if we were arguing. I was embarrassed." He knew he should stop, that he should just zip his lips and not say a word more, but his insides felt raw from walking on eggshells for most of the day. "And I guess we are, because from the moment I woke you up this morning you've been determined to fight with me. Thank God you only ruined my day and not my family's."

"I ruined your day?" Her hands were folded neatly in her lap and she stared straight ahead through the windshield, not even bothering to look his way.

This was the woman he'd made love to, the woman he had wanted to give a special Christmas to. Instead, everything had gone horribly wrong.

"I can honestly say this wasn't how I envisioned us spending Christmas Day together."

"I imagine not." Now she glanced toward him, her eyes full of emotion that he wished was focused on the positive instead of whatever had occupied her mind all day.

"Which means what? That you've deliberately needled me because you didn't want to go with me to my mother's? That you've deliberately undermined our day together?"

Because he'd had that impression all day, but why she'd do that made absolutely no sense to him. No sense whatsoever.

"From the moment of the hospital Christmas party you've refused to listen when I tell you something about myself and you claim it means something else, something that's what you want to hear. Then, when, like today, I'm not what you envisioned, you don't understand why I'm not. Well, hello, Riley, but I am a woman with real needs and real wants and real desires. If I say I like something or don't like something, guess what? That means I like something or don't like something. And you want to know something else?"

"You're obviously going to tell me whether I want to know or not." He pulled his car into his driveway and parked beneath the covered awning.

"I don't like you after all." Trinity jumped out and headed to her car.

He felt a first-class jerk. How had the day gone so wrong? Why was he going after her when it would be better to just let her leave? They had no future. Yet he couldn't let her go.

"Where do you think you're going?" he asked, putting his hand over the car door to prevent her from being able to open it.

"Anywhere you aren't," she spat at him.

"Trinity, why are you doing this?"

Her? Trinity fumed. He was trying to blame this on her? Him and his goody-two-shoes, perfect, rich, Christmas-loving family could just get over themselves. Okay, so she'd liked his family, had enjoyed playing cards with his sisters, mother and aunt, had found herself thinking that this was how families should be. How Christmas should be.

She'd longed to be a real part of his family, had been saddened that she would always be on the outside of such family moments, of real Christmas joy.

But that didn't give Riley reason to blame her for the day going wrong. She'd told him she hadn't wanted to go and he'd finagled her into doing so and then blamed her when things hadn't gone as he'd hoped. Why was that her fault?

She'd taken blame for enough things during her life. For her mother's problems. For her father leaving. For Chase finding her lacking. For Chase leaving her. She refused to take blame any more for not being what someone thought she should be.

"Because I don't want to be here. I don't want to be with you. I didn't from the beginning but I got caught up in this fairy-tale you tried to create. Well, guess what, Riley? Fairy-tales don't exist. They don't come true. Not everyone gets a Prince Charming or a happily-ever-after or even a pair of pink hightops. The whole concept of happily-ever-after is as fake as...as Santa Claus himself."

"You really believe that?"

She nodded, saw the look of disgust in his eyes, the disappointment. No doubt she'd been one big disappointment for him. From last night through today.

"I also believe that I don't want to see you any more. Just leave me alone, please. We're finished." She shoved past him and got into her car.

This time he didn't try to stop her.

CHAPTER THIRTEEN

THROUGH HER TEAR-CRAZED haze, Trinity realized she'd left her cat at Riley's. How could she have forgotten Casper?

Then again, she couldn't exactly be faulted for not thinking rationally. She'd just had a crazy few hours.

She'd had sex, amazing sex that had proved at least on one count Chase had been wrong. She wasn't frigid. She might not be a dynamo in bed, but she at least now knew what all the fuss was about.

She'd met Riley's family. She'd liked them, regretted that she'd probably never see again the wonderful women she'd come to know.

She'd realized she was in love with Riley and then proceeded to fight with him all day.

Christmas. What a blasted day! A day when everything seemed to always go wrong. Only could she really blame everything that had gone wrong today on the holiday?

She'd expected everything to go wrong and had pretty much rejected his sweet, thoughtful gifts. He was right.

She'd been the problem.

How could she have been so blind?

How could she have dirtied something so good? Because Riley was good to her. Good for her. He'd genuinely liked her. Genuinely wanted her. Thinking back to how he'd looked at her, how he'd held her and touched her, she had to wonder if maybe he genuinely loved her.

She'd acted immature, scared, prickly. All because she'd fallen in love and didn't want to be hurt again. In the process she'd been the catalyst that had set the disastrous domino effect into play.

Today she'd been a one-woman demolition crew.

She would see him again. He had her cat. They worked together.

But before she saw him again, she needed to get her head straight. Needed to figure out who she was and what she wanted.

She went up to her apartment, still lost in thought about what she needed to do next. Was she woman enough to trust Riley? To trust in him? Because if she wasn't, then she just needed to let him go, let this be the end rather than continually looking for problems and dragging him down in the process.

If she was woman enough to trust him, if he'd forgive her for today, which was questionable, then what? Where did they go from there?

Distracted, she unlocked her apartment door and stepped inside, only to rub her eyes in disbelief at what she saw.

A nine-foot tree dominated her living room.

A gorgeous tree decorated with twinkling white lights and silver and glass ornaments.

Perhaps he'd meant the angel ornament he'd given her at breakfast to go at the top, but she didn't see how as the tree was amazingly decorated. At the top, brush-

ing against her ceiling, was the silver star they'd seen
at the shopping mall. The one that was so reminiscent
of the one from her childhood classroom when Christmas had been magical to her.

Riley paid attention to details.

She walked over, touched a clear plastic ornament. A
princess ornament. The entire tree was decorated with
various princess paraphernalia. Cartoon princesses. A
pumpkin coach. Tiny glass slippers. A magic wand.
A crown.

A single medium-sized package was under the tree.

How had he done this?

When had he done this?

Last night. When she'd woken up and he hadn't been
there. He'd been here. At her house. Decorating. Trying
to bring the magic of Christmas into her life.

He'd played Santa.

A tear slid down her cheek.

She plopped down on the floor, picked up the package. A tag read, "Don't open until December 25th".

Being careful not to tear the paper, she undid piece
of tape after piece of tape. A shiny silver box was inside. She lifted the lid, moved away white tissue paper.

Her eyes widened at what she saw. "Wow."

She kicked off her shoes. Holding her breath in anticipation, she slipped her foot into one pink hightop
and admired the perfect fit. Oh, yeah, the man paid attention.

"I had to guess your size."

"Riley." She spun towards the door. Her open door.
She'd been so distracted when she'd stepped inside that
she hadn't closed it. He stood there, filling up the doorway with her cat in his arms.

"Sorry, I didn't mean to interrupt, but the door was open."

Her cheeks flushed. With joy that he was there. She didn't need the magic of Christmas in her life.

She needed Riley, because he made every day magic.

He *was* magic.

"You're not interrupting. Not really." Not at all. Never had she been happier to see anyone. Would he think her crazy if she ran and threw herself at him? Wrapped her arms around his neck? Her legs around his waist?

"I brought Casper." He glanced around, looked awkward then set the squirming cat down. Casper took off towards the tree, intent to check out the new items invading her space.

They both watched the cat sniff and check out the tree, the open package, and then settle into the box lid as if it was the most comfortable of beds.

Riley put his hands in his pants pockets. "I won't keep you."

He turned to go. Every fiber of her being screamed to stop him. To risk everything and fight for this man. Whatever came, pain, loss, suffering, a single moment in his arms was worth taking that risk.

"Please do," she called out to his retreating back.

He turned, his forehead wrinkled. "What?"

She stood, took a deep breath. "Please do keep me, Riley."

She wanted him to keep her for ever.

"I don't understand."

She took a step towards him then another, until she stood right in front of him, one shoe on, one shoe off. She stared up into his beautiful blue eyes.

"I want you to keep me, Riley. For ever."

He regarded her for a moment. "What are you saying, Trinity?"

"That I'm an idiot who is so scared that you won't love me, that you will leave me, that I've made it impossible for you to love me and all too probable that you'd leave."

"You pushed me away."

She nodded.

"Why?"

"Because I was scared of how I feel about you."

"Which is?"

"I feel as if I can't breathe when you aren't around."

Some of the tension around his eyes started to ease. "And?"

"And as if I can't breathe when you're around because you take my breath away."

"Keep going," he insisted, crossing his arms over his chest. But his eyes had lost the cloudiness that had hidden away the sparkle she loved. Now that sparkle had come back and gave her strength. If she wanted this, wanted him, she was going to have to confront her fears, not let them overpower her the way they had for the entire day, for years. "You aren't going to make this easy, are you?"

"Lady, when I finally have you admitting that you care about me and want me in your life, you'd better believe that I'm going to keep pushing."

"I…" She shrugged. "I didn't know why you were so nice to me, why you wanted me, why you chose me. I thought maybe I was just another charity case."

"Why wouldn't I choose you? You're everything to me. All day I've kidded myself that we were a mistake, that we should just call it quits, that I could let you go because I'm not a forever kind of man. But from the time you drove away, I knew I couldn't ever call it quits with you." He ran his fingers through his hair. "I don't know what to do, Trinity. I never saw myself as marrying or having kids. Not with my career. I didn't want to be one of those dads." He paused. "I didn't want to be my dad."

"Your dad?" she asked, reeling at all he'd admitted, reeling that he'd said he loved her.

"He worked all the time, was always gone. That's why Christmas is so special to my family. It was the one and only time of the year that my dad didn't work. We had a day of him being with us, playing with us, with us being the center of his attention for an entire day. When the holiday was over, he was back at work and we rarely saw him until the following Christmas. I don't mean to whine. I know I was blessed. He was a good man, provided a good living for his family." Riley shrugged. "It's just that it seemed he was only there as part of our family at Christmas."

"Him working so hard allowed your mother to always be there for you kids, though."

"You're right," Riley agreed. "I know that in my head."

"But in your heart?"

"In my heart, I don't want to be like him."

"Which is?"

"A husband whose wife was lonely. A father whose children longed for his presence. A man I only have good memories of from Christmas."

"I'm sorry," she said, and meant it. "But at least you

do have those memories. And now I understand why Christmas is so important to you, to your family."

Riley nodded. "The first few Christmases after he'd died, my mother was devastated. My brother and sisters and I decided we were going to make sure to always be there for Christmas, to spend a good portion of the day with her, to bring her as much joy as possible."

"I'd say you were a success. She couldn't stop smiling and laughing today."

"But the other woman I wanted to bring as much joy as possible to wasn't smiling and laughing today. Not with me."

She wrapped her arms around his neck, hugged him tightly to her. "I'm sorry, Riley. I was confused, and last night…last night blew me away."

"Last night blew both of us away." He touched her cheek. "I've been doing all the chasing, Trinity, and you've been doing a lot of running." He gestured to her gift. "You said you weren't a glass slipper kind of girl, that you wanted pink hightops so you could run. When you need to run, run to me, Trinity."

Her eyes misted and she put her palms against his face. "It may take me a while to get my head on straight at times, but I will always run to you. You're my star."

He stared down at her in question.

"The star that leads me where I need to be."

He smiled. "I hope so."

She took a deep breath, rested her forehead against his chin. "For however long you want me, I'm yours, Riley."

"Then you're going to be mine for ever." He took her in his arms, kissed her. "Please, don't ever shut me out again the way you did today. My youngest sister could tell I was in love with you. She commented on how much when we were talking today."

That was what his sister had said?

"You told her that you'd made a mistake, that you regretted bringing me."

"You heard that?" He hugged her. "Our timing was off. We needed today, just you and me figuring out what happened last night and making sure we didn't do anything to mess up it happening again and again. But I couldn't cancel Christmas with my family. I just shouldn't have coerced you into going with me."

"I understand. I wouldn't have wanted you to have canceled. As a matter of fact, what I kept thinking was that I wanted what you had. That I wanted to be a part of that family, to experience the warmth and love of what Christmas should be." She stood on tiptoe and pressed a kiss to his lips. "You are what Christmas and love should be."

Riley kissed her long and hard. "My heart is yours, princess. I don't have all the answers to our future, but I'm yours every day for the rest of my life."

Her breath caught. "Really?"

"Really." His eyes catching on something behind her, he swept her up off her feet, carried her over to the tree then sat her down. "There's something I want to do."

Seeing what his gaze had caught on, she knew what he was going to do. Her heart swelled.

He pulled a chair over and she automatically sat down. He dropped to one knee and picked up the other hightop.

"Thank you for this." She spread out her arms towards the tree. "You make a great Santa."

He shook his head. "Wrong guy."

She arched a brow, not quite sure what he meant.

"I'm not going for Santa in your life."

"What are you going for in my life?"

He grinned and slipped the other shoe onto her foot. "I'm your Prince Charming, of course. Your right Prince Charming."

"My one and only Prince Charming," she assured him, touching his arm.

"I like the sound of that."

"But, Riley, I should tell you."

"Yes?"

"You're my Santa, too."

"Oh?"

She nodded. "Every day I'm with you is like Christmas."

"You're the one who is a gift, princess. You've made my life better."

"Hey, I have a gift for you, too," she recalled, jumping up and rushing to the drawer where she'd stashed his gift.

Smiling, she handed him the bag.

He eyed it suspiciously. "You used a bag rather than wrapping paper?"

She grinned. "I bought this before my wrapping lesson."

He pulled out the paper and lifted out a box about the size of his hand. What was inside made him burst out laughing.

And had his eyes shining brightly.

"It's perfect."

"I thought you'd think so, snowflake."

Holding the ornament as if it was the most precious

treasure, he smiled at her, love in his eyes. "I love you, Trinity."

Her heart swelled with Christmas joy, with love. She leaned forward and planted a kiss on his lips. "I love you, too. Thank you for my best Christmas ever."

He grinned. "Until next year's."

EPILOGUE

CHRISTMAS DAY A year later, Trinity wasn't so sure Riley had topped the previous year's Christmas. As a matter of fact, at the moment she wasn't even sure she liked him. Or that she'd ever allow him to touch her again.

She moaned with pain.

There was just something about this day.

"Come on, sweetheart, you're almost there."

Okay, so she probably would let him. After all, she did love him with all her heart and was loved by all of his heart.

"Breathe, honey."

She was breathing. Trinity grimaced at her husband, who dabbed at her sweaty face with a washcloth. Her calm, patient, always-positive husband who had brought so much joy into her life. So much happiness. So much security and magic.

He'd given her Christmas.

And so much more.

"When the next contraction hits," the obstetrician said, "and when I tell you, I want you to push as hard as you can."

She felt as if she'd been pushing for hours, but in reality not that much time had gone by. She'd woken up during the middle of Christmas Eve night, had found Riley missing from bed and had gone to look for him. Not surprisingly, she'd found him beneath their Christmas tree, playing Santa.

What had been surprising was that before she'd been able to say anything she'd felt a gush of liquid between her legs. A gush of amniotic fluid as her waters had broken.

According to the clock on the wall, it was barely nine on Christmas morning. She was in the hospital. With her husband, The pink hightops she'd insisted on wearing digging into the stirrups. With their soon-to-be-born baby on its way. And their family anxious in the waiting area. The entire Williams clan.

"Push, Trinity," Riley encouraged, clasping her hand and focusing on her. "Look at me and push."

She tried to look at him but kept squeezing her eyes closed in pain as she attempted to turn her insides out.

"Breathe, baby. Breathe."

Breathe. Push. Pant.

Trinity felt a gut-wrenching pain then horrendous pressure.

"The baby's head is out," the doctor praised. "There's lots of hair."

Another contraction, a few more pushes and Trinity cried.

"You have a baby girl," the obstetrician informed them. "Congratulations."

"A girl." Riley said the words with absolute wonder. "We have a daughter."

Exhausted, but amazed at the man smiling at her with all the love a man had ever felt for any woman shining in his eyes, Trinity nodded. "A girl, born on Christmas Day."

"The most precious gift anyone has ever given me."

Trinity tried to point out that Riley was the one who'd given her the precious gift of their daughter.

"Joy Noelle Williams."

Trinity glanced down at the baby in her arms. "I have this feeling that my role as princess is going to be booted by this little sweetheart." She smiled at the man who'd brought so much joy into her life. Who'd made her part of his family, given her a family of her own. "I think you may have a hard time topping this year."

"Perhaps in your delicate condition you've forgotten, but I'm a man who aims to please, so just you wait and see."

Her eyes widened because she recognized that determined look on his face.

He just grinned. "Merry Christmas, darling."

* * * * *

Mills & Boon® Hardback

December 2013

ROMANCE

Defiant in the Desert	Sharon Kendrick
Not Just the Boss's Plaything	Caitlin Crews
Rumours on the Red Carpet	Carole Mortimer
The Change in Di Navarra's Plan	Lynn Raye Harris
The Prince She Never Knew	Kate Hewitt
His Ultimate Prize	Maya Blake
More than a Convenient Marriage?	Dani Collins
A Hunger for the Forbidden	Maisey Yates
The Reunion Lie	Lucy King
The Most Expensive Night of Her Life	Amy Andrews
Second Chance with Her Soldier	Barbara Hannay
Snowed in with the Billionaire	Caroline Anderson
Christmas at the Castle	Marion Lennox
Snowflakes and Silver Linings	Cara Colter
Beware of the Boss	Leah Ashton
Too Much of a Good Thing?	Joss Wood
After the Christmas Party...	Janice Lynn
Date with a Surgeon Prince	Meredith Webber

MEDICAL

From Venice with Love	Alison Roberts
Christmas with Her Ex	Fiona McArthur
Her Mistletoe Wish	Lucy Clark
Once Upon a Christmas Night...	Annie Claydon

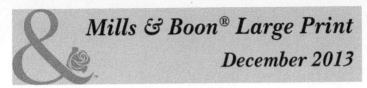

Mills & Boon® Large Print
December 2013

ROMANCE

The Billionaire's Trophy	Lynne Graham
Prince of Secrets	Lucy Monroe
A Royal Without Rules	Caitlin Crews
A Deal with Di Capua	Cathy Williams
Imprisoned by a Vow	Annie West
Duty at What Cost?	Michelle Conder
The Rings That Bind	Michelle Smart
A Marriage Made in Italy	Rebecca Winters
Miracle in Bellaroo Creek	Barbara Hannay
The Courage To Say Yes	Barbara Wallace
Last-Minute Bridesmaid	Nina Harrington

HISTORICAL

Not Just a Governess	Carole Mortimer
A Lady Dares	Bronwyn Scott
Bought for Revenge	Sarah Mallory
To Sin with a Viking	Michelle Willingham
The Black Sheep's Return	Elizabeth Beacon

MEDICAL

NYC Angels: Making the Surgeon Smile	Lynne Marshall
NYC Angels: An Explosive Reunion	Alison Roberts
The Secret in His Heart	Caroline Anderson
The ER's Newest Dad	Janice Lynn
One Night She Would Never Forget	Amy Andrews
When the Cameras Stop Rolling...	Connie Cox

Mills & Boon® *Hardback*

January 2014

ROMANCE

The Dimitrakos Proposition	Lynne Graham
His Temporary Mistress	Cathy Williams
A Man Without Mercy	Miranda Lee
The Flaw in His Diamond	Susan Stephens
Forged in the Desert Heat	Maisey Yates
The Tycoon's Delicious Distraction	Maggie Cox
A Deal with Benefits	Susanna Carr
The Most Expensive Lie of All	Michelle Conder
The Dance Off	Ally Blake
Confessions of a Bad Bridesmaid	Jennifer Rae
The Greek's Tiny Miracle	Rebecca Winters
The Man Behind the Mask	Barbara Wallace
English Girl in New York	Scarlet Wilson
The Final Falcon Says I Do	Lucy Gordon
Mr (Not Quite) Perfect	Jessica Hart
After the Party	Jackie Braun
Her Hard to Resist Husband	Tina Beckett
Mr Right All Along	Jennifer Taylor

MEDICAL

The Rebel Doc Who Stole Her Heart	Susan Carlisle
From Duty to Daddy	Sue MacKay
Changed by His Son's Smile	Robin Gianna
Her Miracle Twins	Margaret Barker

Mills & Boon® Large Print

January 2014

ROMANCE

HISTORICAL

MEDICAL

1213 GEN STD LP